A WOLF IN SHEEP'S CLOTHING

Longarm had not reached the end of the block before he heard someone hurrying along behind him, the footsteps light and rapid. He stopped and turned only to find that the pedestrian was a woman.

She was shabbily clothed, her dress drab and in need of washing. She had a shawl draped over her shoulders, and her hair was disheveled, flyaway wisps of it coming undone from her bun and giving her an even more unkempt appearance as did a smudge of something dark—old makeup or simply dirt—on her right cheek.

"Do you have a light, mister?"

"A light?"

"A match, I mean. Do you have a match?"

"I reckon I do have a match that I'd be pleased t' give you." He dipped two fingers into his vest pocket to extract the requested lucifer.

While Longarm was occupied with that, the woman's right hand flashed out of her pocket.

He saw the glint of lamplight on steel and jerked backward barely in time to avoid having his throat slashed . . .

DON'T MISS THESE
ALL-ACTION WESTERN SERIES
FROM THE BERKLEY PUBLISHING GROUP

THE GUNSMITH *by J. R. Roberts*
Clint Adams was a legend among lawmen, outlaws, and ladies. They called him . . . the Gunsmith.

LONGARM *by Tabor Evans*
The popular long-running series about Deputy U.S. Marshal Long—his life, his loves, his fight for justice.

SLOCUM *by Jake Logan*
Today's longest-running action Western. John Slocum rides a deadly trail of hot blood and cold steel.

BUSHWHACKERS *by B. J. Lanagan*
An action-packed series by the creators of Longarm! The rousing adventures of the most brutal gang of cutthroats ever assembled—Quantrill's Raiders.

DIAMONDBACK *by Guy Brewer*
Dex Yancey is Diamondback, a Southern gentleman turned con man when his brother cheats him out of the family fortune. Ladies love him. Gamblers hate him. But nobody pulls one over on Dex . . .

WILDGUN *by Jack Hanson*
The blazing adventures of mountain man Will Barlow—from the creators of Longarm!

TEXAS TRACKER *by Tom Calhoun*
Meet J.T. Law: the most relentless—and dangerous—manhunter in all Texas. Where sheriffs and posses fail, he's the best man to bring in the most vicious outlaws—for a price.

TABOR EVANS

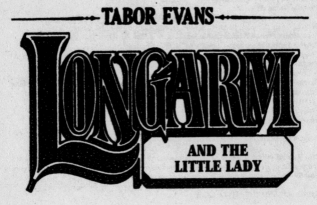

LONGARM

AND THE LITTLE LADY

JOVE BOOKS, NEW YORK

THE BERKLEY PUBLISHING GROUP
Published by the Penguin Group
Penguin Group (USA) Inc.
375 Hudson Street, New York, New York 10014, USA
Penguin Group (Canada), 10 Alcorn Avenue, Toronto, Ontario M4V 3B2, Canada
(a division of Pearson Penguin Canada Inc.)
Penguin Books Ltd., 80 Strand, London WC2R ORL, England
Penguin Group Ireland, 25 St. Stephen's Green, Dublin 2, Ireland (a division of Penguin Books Ltd.)
Penguin Group (Australia), 250 Camberwell Road, Camberwell, Victoria 3124, Australia
(a division of Pearson Australia Group Pty. Ltd.)
Penguin Books India Pvt. Ltd., 11 Community Centre, Panchsheel Park, New Delhi—110 017, India
Penguin Group (NZ), Cnr. Airborne and Rosedale Roads, Albany, Auckland 1310, New Zealand
(a division of Pearson New Zealand Ltd.)
Penguin Books (South Africa) (Pty.) Ltd., 24 Sturdee Avenue, Rosebank, Johannesburg 2196,
South Africa

Penguin Books Ltd., Registered Offices: 80 Strand, London WC2R ORL, England

This is a work of fiction. Names, characters, places, and incidents either are the product of the author's imagination or are used fictitiously, and any resemblance to actual persons, living or dead, business establishments, events, or locales is entirely coincidental.

LONGARM AND THE LITTLE LADY

A Jove Book / published by arrangement with the author

PRINTING HISTORY
Jove edition / August 2005

Copyright © 2005 by The Berkley Publishing Group

ISBN: 0-515-13987-4

JOVE®
Jove Books are published by The Berkley Publishing Group,
a division of Penguin Group (USA) Inc.,
375 Hudson Street, New York, New York 10014.
JOVE is a registered trademark of Penguin Group (USA) Inc.
The "J" design is a trademark belonging to Penguin Group (USA) Inc.

PRINTED IN THE UNITED STATES OF AMERICA

10 9 8 7 6 5 4 3 2 1

Chapter 1

Two days of riding on the damn train left Longarm feeling like he'd been doused in soot, cinders and coal dust. He needed a bath and a drink—maybe not in that order—and the sooner he got them the better.

The door at the front of the passenger coach opened and the conductor came in, walking with a seaman's roll, seemingly unmindful of the swaying and shaking of the car.

"Omaha, folks. End of the line coming up. Everybody out at Omaha or stay aboard and go right on back to Californy, whichever you please. Next stop Omaha, folks. All out at Omaha."

The conductor passed on through to the next coach back, and Longarm dipped into his vest pocket for the railroad grade Ingersoll watch he carried there. The train was right on time. At least that was something that was going right.

Not that this assignment was going badly. It was going just fine, thank you. It was just that this was a piece-of-shit assignment to begin with.

You would think that U.S. Marshal Billy Vail's best deputy would be given a job more interesting than transporting some nobody of a prisoner. But he wasn't.

Billy, damn him, had explained that Longarm was chosen because once he got the asshole down to Fort Smith Longarm would be expected to stick around to testify against the man. It was just Longarm's bad luck that he'd been aboard the train that day when this jasper blew up the mail car and escaped with a sack of letters in addition to the contents of the safe, killing a railroad detective and a postal inspector in the process. Bad luck, too, that Longarm looked out the coach window in time that day to see the robber making his getaway on a horse that was being held for him in a nearby thicket.

Now a county sheriff in Wisconsin had the fugitive in custody waiting to turn the man over to the federal authorities so he could be given a fair and impartial trial . . . before the son of a bitch was hanged by the neck until dead.

Longarm returned his watch to the vest pocket and waited patiently for the clacking, rattling coach to come to a hissing stop, then waited a little longer for the other passengers to grab their things and file out. Finally he stood and made his way to the end of the coach and down the steel steps to the platform.

He strolled back to the baggage car to collect his carpetbag, Winchester carbine and saddle, waving off a porter's attempts to give assistance that was not needed.

"The Grant," he said as he climbed into an empty cab that was waiting outside the depot. The Grant was his favorite hotel in Omaha. Not only did they have comfortable accommodations, their dining room was among the finest eateries in the city. And the bar stocked Longarm's favorite brand of Maryland rye whiskey, too. It was a combination he could never resist when he was in the city.

He made himself comfortable on the leather upholstered seat of the hansom—infinitely more comfortable than the rough mohair of the Union Pacific coach had been—and in less than ten minutes was standing at the Grant's front desk.

"Good afternoon, Mr. Long. So nice to see you again, sir. Would you like the same room, sir?"

"That'd be fine."

"And how long will you be with us this visit, sir?"

"That's kinda up to you. I want you to arrange passage for me on a steamboat downriver to St. Louis, then back up the Mississippi to a place called Ferryville."

"We will be happy to do that for you, Mr. Long."

"Thanks."

"Earliest departure possible?"

Longarm grinned. "Earliest after I've had time to get a bath anyway."

"Of course, sir. I will send a tub and hot water to your room at once."

"Send a bottle and glass up, too, I reckon. That good rye you always have here."

"More than one glass, perhaps?" the desk clerk suggested.

"One should oughta do it." His grin flashed again. "Unless somethin' changes real sudden."

The clerk laughed. "I will send two then. Just in case"

"Thanks."

The clerk snapped his fingers and a bellboy appeared at Longarm's side as if by magic. "Take the gentleman's things to number thirty-one, Jimmy."

Longarm gave the kid credit. He didn't show any disappointment even though 31 was third floor rear, overlooking the distant Missouri.

"Let us know if there is anything else we can do for you, Mr. Long."

"Will do. Thanks." Longarm followed the skinny bellhop upstairs and tipped the kid a whole dime for the help, then told him, "Wait here a minute while I get outa these clothes. I'll want everything washed and ironed right away since I don't know how long I'll be stayin' before my boat leaves."

"Yes, sir."

Longarm barely had time enough to give the bellboy his shirt, socks and underthings before a trio of other, more muscular bellboys were at the door with buckets of water and a copper-lined slipper tub, and a few minutes after that he was chest deep in steaming hot water with his hair lathered and a cheroot between his teeth.

So far, he thought, this assignment was not going quite as bad as he'd expected.

Chapter 2

Now *that* would make any trip worthwhile. Longarm laid his knife and fork down and concentrated on the view rather than on the juicy steak he'd been working on.

The young woman three tables over was oblivious to him and to the other diners in the room, but Longarm could scarcely take his eyes from her. She was porcelain and lace. A vision come alive. Rosebud mouth and high, rounded cheeks. Straight nose and delicately slender neck. One wisp of golden hair escaped from the prim bun at the nape of her neck to curl softly in front of her ear.

She was thin, with an impossibly small waist and practically no tits, but that could be excused as a function of youth. He guessed she was fifteen or sixteen, seventeen at the outside, anyway, old enough for marriage but certainly not old enough to be traveling alone. Yet she sat alone at her table, eyes demurely focused on her plate while all around her gave their attention to this exquisitely beautiful lass.

Longarm could not speak for the other gentlemen in the Grant's dining room, but as for himself when he looked at this beautiful girl what he felt was not lust but—most unusual for him—a desire to protect and care for her.

He felt—good Lord!—he felt *fatherly* toward her. Damn. The realization struck him so hard he dropped his fork. It clattered off the side of his plate, bounded into the stem of his water goblet and then fell noisily to the floor. Half the heads in the room turned toward him, including that of the lovely young woman those few yards distant.

Longarm felt his cheeks burn and quickly became annoyed with himself because of it. He was being silly, dammit. An old fool, never mind that he wasn't all that old. It was just . . . well . . . there was something about this girl that was very special. She aroused feelings in him that were decidedly out of the ordinary.

He bent to retrieve the fork, but a waiter was already there, whisking the soiled implement away and placing a fresh one beside his plate.

"Thanks," Longarm mumbled. Not that the waiter was really paying any attention. He, too, was surreptitiously staring at the girl. Probably, Longarm guessed, the dining room staff was all competing for any opportunity to wait upon the girl's slightest needs.

Hell, Longarm didn't blame them. Given the chance, he would be right in there with them, elbowing others aside so he could be the one to fetch water or tea or a sweet for her pleasure. And all with no thought but to please and to serve.

Damned strange effect she was having on him, but there it was. Made him wonder if he was getting old, it did.

Longarm's face remained impassive, but inwardly he began to smile. At himself. Old? Not damn hardly. There was just something about that girl, that was all. Not that it mattered. She was just a stranger passing on the street, so to speak. Another diner in a public eatery, each obviously traveling, coming together under one roof by chance, never destined to meet or to speak or to so much as see each other again.

But she surely was pretty.

6

The girl finished her meal, daintily wiped her lips and began to rise. Immediately there were two waiters ready to help her with her chair and to bow her out of the dining room, every head in the place turning to watch her progress.

She walked with a severe limp, Longarm saw, giving her an awkward side-to-side gait as if one leg were considerably shorter than the other. Whatever the cause, it was not recent, for she seemed quite oblivious to it. A recent injury might have made her self-conscious, but she carried herself as if she were unaware that she even had it.

That small imperfection notwithstanding, Longarm thought she was about as pretty a thing as he'd seen. Ever. And that was saying quite a mouthful.

He watched, in no hurry at all, until the girl was out of the room and he could no longer see her, before going back to his meal. He was not the only one in the room to do so either.

Finally, once she had disappeared into the lobby, Longarm and all the other diners resumed their interrupted meals.

While he finished his steak, Longarm gave thought to the question of whether he wanted to sit in on a few hands of poker tonight or settle for a cigar, a drink and an early night's sleep. The girl, pretty though she had been, was quickly forgotten.

Chapter 3

"Oh, Mr. Long. Good morning, sir. I have your transportation arrangements, sir."

Longarm turned away from the dining room, where he'd intended to have breakfast, and crossed the lobby to the desk where the clerk was smiling rather slyly. More than a steamboat ticket would call for, Longarm thought.

"Good morning. You got me booked, I take it?"

"Yes, sir, I did. And, well, you may be interested to know that you have a secret admirer."

"Really? I don't recall tellin' anybody I'd be here, and I haven't talked to anybody since I got here except you and the staff."

"I would be glad to tell you the identity of this person, sir, but I am sworn to secrecy."

"Goodness, that sounds important."

The clerk smiled. "Oh, I suppose not. It is all perfectly innocent, I assure you. This, um, person merely thought you cut quite the fine figure and asked who you are. I hope you don't mind if I mentioned a little of your reputation to he—to this person, I mean. As I say, it is all quite innocent and aboveboard."

"Then no harm is done, I reckon." Longarm grinned.

9

"Sure wish you'da sent her up to my room last night. A body can catch his death of cold sleeping alone in one of them big beds of yours."

"I trust your health survived the night, Marshal. But really, this party is not the sort to have, um, casual encounters. I am quite certain of that."

"Drat," Longarm said with another grin. "What I coulda used is the other kind."

"Ha ha, yes, sir, indeed, sir."

"You were sayin' about my boat ticket?" Longarm reminded the fellow.

"Yes, indeed. I've booked you with the Templeton agency. They are brokers for several top-notch boats, don't you see. They have you . . . just a moment, I have it written down here somewhere . . . ah, here it is." He pulled out a slip of paper and read from it before handing it across to Longarm.

"You leave at eleven-thirty this morning aboard the *Sacagawea,* bound downriver for St. Louis. Once you are there, you will transfer to the *Willis Adams* for the trip north on the Mississippi to, um, let me see here. Oh, yes. Ferryville, Wisconsin. I suggest once you get aboard you remind the purser to make a stop at the landing there. I doubt they would normally be scheduled to call there."

"Right, thanks."

"I know the *Sacagawea* and it is a fine boat. A sternwheeler. Excellent crew and accommodation. I think you will be more than pleased."

"You've done good, friend. Thanks."

"We are always glad to be of service, Marshal."

Longarm reached into his pocket and pulled out a silver cartwheel which happened to be a Mexican peso, the equivalent of an American dollar and accepted as such pretty much anywhere. He slid it across the counter to the clerk and watched the coin disappear into the man's pocket as if by magic.

"Thank you, sir. You are very kind."

"Do I need a ticket or anything?"

"The broker is sending those this morning. I expect to have them in hand before you check out."

"All right then." Longarm grinned. "If my secret admirer comes around again, I'll be in the dining room having breakfast."

"Ah, if only I had not faithfully promised my silence," the clerk mused with a sad shake of his head.

"Don't worry about it. You say it's innocent stuff, so I reckon there wouldn't be nothin' gained by knowing anyhow."

"Yes, sir. Quite true."

"I'll be back down around ten or so. Could you have a hansom ready for me then, please?"

"Yes, sir, Mr. Long. It will be my pleasure."

Longarm tapped the brim of his Stetson with a forefinger and ambled off toward the dining room. He was hankering after bacon this morning. And biscuits. They made a fine biscuit at the Grant.

Chapter 4

The *Sacagawea* was no queen of the river. A baroness at best, but certainly no queen, and hadn't been on the day she first went into service. And that had been a good fair number of years ago from the looks of her. Now she was a little the worse for wear, with ancient stains on her hull and flaking paint.

One of the crown-shaped spark arresters on her right-hand stack—Longarm tried to remember the nautical term for that side and thought it was starboard but was not positive; the crown thing he was sure of, those were called "feathers" for reasons that quite escaped him—had been knocked askew so that the *Sacagawea* looked like she was a little bit drunk. Or jaunty. Better to think of her as being cheerfully jaunty than tipsy, he decided.

She was three stories—decks, that would be—tall and perhaps two hundred or so feet long, not counting the sternwheel that extended behind like the tail on a slightly bedraggled rooster.

Longarm paused on the quay to give the old boat a looking over, then stepped toward the gangplank that would take him aboard.

"Take yo bag, suh?"

"I can handle it, thanks."

"Please, suh?"

Longarm glanced at the huge black man who was standing there with one hand extended for Longarm's carpetbag. The fellow was lumpy with muscle and glistening with sweat. He stood a good three or four inches taller than Longarm and probably outweighed him by sixty pounds or more. He looked like he had been carrying heavy crates and bales since the break of day. No doubt the lightweight carpetbag would be a relief after the burdens he'd been under all morning.

"Y'know, come to think of it I reckon I could use some help with this bag now that you mention it."

"Yes, suh, thank you, suh." The handle of the carpetbag was barely large enough to contain the stevedore's ham-sized fist. He took the bag with one hand and with the other dragged a bandana from his back pocket to quickly mop his face. "Right behind you, suh."

Longarm strode across the gangplank and stopped to check in with the purser or whoever the little fellow was who was consulting a list as the passengers came aboard by ones and twos. Longarm gave his name to the man.

"Oh, yes. A late booking, I see, going only as far as St. Louis. Cabin eleven, Mr. Long. You will find it on the lower deck at the stern. Show the gent where his cabin is, Rastus."

"Yes, suh, Mr. Parker, suh."

Longarm might not know all that much about boats and nautical shit, but he could figure out front from back. Now, the stern, that was at the back. He led the way along the railed passage that ran completely around the structure. His cabin was probably the least desirable of the several dozen aboard, back where it would be assaulted by the constant slap of paddles on water and the chuff and chug of the engine room a few feet away.

Not that that should matter so very much. He would be aboard less than forty-eight hours and intended to spend most of his time in the salon playing cards. There were bound to be some other gentlemen aboard who enjoyed the pasteboards.

"This looks like the place," Longarm said when he came to number 11. He turned and took the bag from the stevedore. "D'you mind if I ask you something?"

"No, suh, you ast whatever you like."

"Is your name really Rastus?"

The big man grinned. "No, suh, you know it ain't. My name's Benjamin Sipes, suh."

"It's a pleasure to meet you, Benjamin. Thanks for carrying my gear." Longarm pulled a nickel from his pocket and offered it to Sipes.

"Thank you, suh, but you the one done me the favor, givin' me a break like that. I couldn't take yo money, Mistuh Long, suh."

"All right then, Benjamin. Thank you very much."

"Thank *you*, suh." Sipes touched his forehead and headed back toward the quay, his broad shoulders filling the passageway.

Longarm went inside his temporary home to see just how cramped and dreary the cabin would prove to be.

Longarm reached into his coat pocket for a cheroot, then frowned when he failed to find one. "Damn," he muttered, pushing his chair back from the card table. "I'll sit out for now if you don't mind, gentlemen. I have to go down to my cabin for something. I expect I'll be back later."

"Shall we save your seat, Mr. Long?" one of the card players offered, a bearded congenial sort named Hirt.

"Not if someone else comes along who wants it; otherwise I'll be back to claim it in a little while," Longarm told Hirt and the other three seated around the table.

Hirt smiled. "Anytime between now and when we dock at Vicksburg. I don't know about you, but my cabin is too small to bother with except by true necessity."

"I know what you mean," Longarm agreed as he gathered up the handful of coins in front of him and dropped them into his pocket without counting to see if he was ahead so far or behind. He grinned. "I haven't tried turning around inside it, but I just might have to step outside to do that."

"We shall see you later then, Mr. Long," a man named Dwyer said. "You can help us skin my good friend Douglas here." Dwyer reached for the deck and began shuffling.

The game was draw poker; the play was desultory, and the stakes were low. All the gents were playing to pass the time and enjoy a little company while the *Sacagawea* made her way downriver. Winning or losing was not the issue.

Longarm retrieved his Stetson from a rack beside the lounge door and stepped out into the cool night air on the uppermost deck. He felt pretty good actually. Supper had been passing fair and sat warm and comfortable in his belly. The play of the cards and the company of the other gentlemen was pleasant. And in less than two days they should tie up at St. Louis and he could begin the next leg of his journey.

He took the two flights of stairs—well, he insisted on thinking of them as stairs, dammit, even though he understood that on a boat they were properly called ladders—down to the main deck, where his undersized cabin was.

There was a constant hiss of steam and groan of machinery and always the pounding slap of the paddles biting into the dark water of the great Missouri.

Despite the noise back here at his cabin, Longarm could think of worse ways to travel than in the comfort of a riverboat, even a second-class boat like this one.

He paused outside the door of number 11 to search through his pockets for the key.

"I'm gonna have your ass thrown off this boat, nigger," he heard from somewhere nearby. "You ain't gonna work on the river again. Time I get done with you there won't nobody hire you again. You hear me, nigger? I'll see to that."

"Please, suh, don' do that. Please." The second voice sounded familiar.

The voices were followed by the sound of flesh striking flesh and an angry snarl.

Jesus, Longarm thought. If Benjamin Sipes hit somebody, he might knock the fellow's head clean off his shoulders. Longarm hoped that was not what he'd just heard. He stuffed his key back into his pocket and followed the sound of the voices around to the tiny platform at the extreme back end of the boat, overlooking the churning paddles.

Dripping water gleamed silver in the moonlight as it streamed off the revolving paddles, and back there the sound of the machinery was loud.

Longarm saw Sipes standing with his hands at his sides, making no move to defend himself, while a gentleman—Longarm used that term very loosely—drew back a fist and punched Benjamin square in his already bloody face. The burly stevedore, who surely could have snapped the man's spine in two with a twist of his big hands, took the abuse without flinching. It must have taken a heap of discipline for him to do that without fighting back, Longarm thought. Longarm would have given the arrogant bastard cause to regret those punches if this man or any other tried to hit him.

But then a black man working on a riverboat could expect nothing in the way of fairness in any dispute with a passenger. Benjamin would be the one seen to be in the wrong no matter the truth.

The passenger, leaner than Benjamin but almost as tall, drew back his fist again.

This had gone just damn near far enough, Longarm thought.

He took a step forward just as the passenger's fist lashed out toward Benjamin's unprotected face.

Chapter 5

Longarm's hand flashed out to snag the fellow's fist in midair well before it reached its intended target. "Whoa, mister. You keep this up and you're like to get blood all over the deck."

"Who the hell are you?" the passenger demanded.

Longarm turned loose of the man's fist and gave him a thin smile that held not the least hint of mirth or friendliness in it. He inclined his head toward the still-silent and motionless Benjamin. "I'm a friend of his. And while he can't defend himself, mister, I damn sure can. My advice to you would be for you to back away and go crawl into whatever hole you slithered out of. D'you understand me?"

Slowly, carefully enunciating one word at a time, Longarm added, "Go . . . away . . . right . . . fucking . . . now."

"You can't tell me what to do, damn you."

"Mistuh Long, suh, please don' you be getting' yoself in no trouble on account o' me, suh, please," Benjamin said in a worried voice.

"The nig is giving you good advice," the passenger said. "You should take it or I will whip your ass."

Longarm grinned. "That's easy enough to say. Doing it might be another thing, mister. D'you really want to try?"

"Look, I didn't come down here looking for a fight. This nigger was giving me some lip. I don't have to take that. I won't take any shit off a human person, much less some nigger. You're a white man. You know what I mean."

"I know what you mean all right. You're the kind of slime who likes to beat up on people who can't fight back. It makes you feel like a man, and that's something you never will be. Well, mister, I *can* fight back if you want to start anything. So you think it over real careful and do whatever pleases you, but keep in mind that Mr. Sipes here is a friend of mine. You aren't. If you make any trouble for him . . . with the captain or with anybody else . . . I will stomp you flat and toss you overboard. Are we clear on this, mister? Is there any doubt in your feeble little mind? Leave him the fuck be or I will rip your lips off and use 'em for a hatband. Now get out of here. And don't bother this man again."

The passenger stood for a long moment glowering at Longarm and inwardly fuming. His complexion turned dark. The man was boiling mad and Longarm could practically see steam rising out of his ears.

Longarm halfway hoped the fellow would take him up on the challenge. It would be a pleasure to give him a lesson in manners.

The moment passed, though. Longarm could as good as see the man's resolve deflate and wither away. The tension in his shoulders faded and he no longer looked Longarm in the eye. He was beaten without Longarm having to throw a single punch.

"You just made a big mistake," the passenger snarled, blustering and threatening now only to keep from admitting defeat. "I'll let you off easy this one time just because one stinking nigger isn't worth a fuss. But you stay out of my way from now on. Do you hear me? You stay clear of me."

"The only time I'd worry about you, mister, is when my back is turned, you yellow son of a bitch."

A spark of anger flashed in the man's eyes. But only for a moment. He was whipped, whether he wanted to admit it or not.

After a few seconds he turned and pushed past Benjamin in a hasty escape to the passageway on the port side of the boat.

"Are you all right?" Longarm asked Benjamin.

"Yes, suh, but you shouldn't ought to . . ."

"Hush with that crap. You could've torn him apart, and all three of us knew it. Just like we all three know why you didn't. I just hope he won't cause any more trouble for you."

"I don' think he will, suh. Not 'less he cooks up some good lies first." Benjamin pulled a rag from his hip pocket and used it to mop some of the blood off his face and neck. "That man, he wanted him some black meat. Seen a pretty little gal that works in the galley an' cleans in the cabins an' such. He come to me wantin' me t' take her t' his cabin, you see. She a married lady, Mistuh Long, suh. I couldn't do nothing like that. I tol' him so an' he got real mad." Benjamin chuckled. "But he ain't gonna tell the captain 'bout wantin' a piece o' nigger pussy. No, suh, he ain't gonna say nothing like that an' tell on hisself."

"Would you do me a favor, Benjamin?"

"Mistuh Long, I do anything you ast me to. Anything."

"If that man gives you any trouble or tries to get you in trouble with the boat's officers, I want you to tell me about it."

"Oh, I couldn't . . ."

"You said anything. Did you mean that?"

"Yes, suh, you knows I did."

"Then that's what I'm asking. If he gives you anymore trouble at all, you tell me about it. Please."

"Yes, suh. Thank you, suh."

"Then if you will excuse me, Benjamin, I need to get some cigars from my cabin," he grinned, "then go back upstairs and clean out those gents I've been playing cards with."

21

"Yes, suh. I hope you does just that, suh," Benjamin said, his smile broad and cheerful.

Longarm turned away without another thought for the asshole who had been bullying Benjamin.

Chapter 6

Longarm sat trying to remember what you called these puffy, fluffy, Frenchified omelet things. Dammit anyhow. Why'd they have to take a perfectly honest egg and screw around with it like this? Seemed like anytime you called a cook a chef he had to fancy things up until you couldn't hardly recognize them.

Not that this here . . . whatever it was . . . was bad, mind you. It tasted all right. But plain old fried eggs and fried potatoes and maybe a pork chop or slab of steak, now that was a proper breakfast.

Longarm scowled and carved off a little hunk of the airy and insubstantial egg concoction.

His expression changed when he looked up and saw what was waltzing in through the dining salon doors. It was that same marvelous creature who had been at the Grant back in Omaha. She was wearing the same bottle green traveling gown that she'd had on then. And just as at the Grant, when the girl entered the room every man's eyes were on her, some hungrily and some protectively, but all admiring her delicate beauty.

She seemed unaware of all that, just as she seemed unaware of the limp that gave her that halting, side-to-side

23

gait. She was . . . Longarm searched for the word he wanted . . . The young woman was not merely beautiful— although she was also that—she was serene. That was it. Serene. Marvelous.

The lucky waiter whose turn it was to serve her hurried to escort her to a table and hold the chair for her. Any and every man in the place would gladly have done the same. And then some.

Longarm smiled a little to himself, not even minding now the foo-foo way they fancied up the foods on board. He absently carved another sliver of baked egg stuff off the side of the . . . *soufflé,* that was it. The fancy omelets were called soufflés. But tomorrow, he thought, he'd see if he could get plain old scrambled eggs and a mess of potatoes instead.

Tomorrow he'd want to take his breakfast at the same time as the little lady across the way again, too. The sight of her seemed a mighty fine way for a man to start his day. Why he—

"Sir? Excuse me, sir." A gent in a ship's company uniform stood beside Longarm's table. Behind him was the asshole who'd been abusing Benjamin Sipes last evening. "I am sorry to bother you, sir, but there is a, um, well, there is a complaint, you see. About your conduct on board. I understand you, well, I am told that you assaulted this gentleman last night. You threatened him, I believe. With bodily harm. Is that correct, sir? Did you threaten to beat him up like he says you did?"

Longarm carefully folded his napkin and laid it beside his plate, then pushed his chair back a few feet.

"Watch him," the cowardly passenger said, quickly stepping to the side so as to place the ship's officer between himself and Longarm. "He is a violent man. Don't trust him." The passenger was big, a little taller than Longarm, and appeared to be well set up. The ship's officer was half a head shorter and rather thin. But the passenger sought

24

shelter behind the smaller man. The officer appeared not to notice.

"Please, sir. Do not cause a commotion. Just please, would you mind answering my question?"

Longarm laced his fingers together across his belly. That happened by coincidence to place his hands very close to the grips of the big Colt .44–40 that rode in a cross-draw holster beside his belt buckle.

"If you are asking, sir, did I strike this piece of shit, I did not. Should have maybe, but I didn't. Now, as far as threats go, I wouldn't say that I threatened him neither. What I did was make him a promise. If he bothered me or this friend o' mine . . . Did he tell you about that part of it, by the way? I'm betting he forgot to mention that he was beatin' up on somebody when I came along . . . but I could be mistaken about that, I suppose. Anyway, what I done was to make him a promise. I told him I'd beat hell outa him and throw him overboard if he caused anymore trouble."

Longarm grinned. "What d'you think, mister? Would you say this is trouble, this here little talk we're having? D'you think maybe I should keep my promise to this useless sack of dog turds?"

"Sir, I . . . I . . . You cannot talk to people that way," the officer babbled, an expression of shock and horror pulling at his face. "Really, sir. I . . . we may have to ask you to leave at our next stop if you persist in this belligerent attitude."

Longarm nodded slowly, thoughtfully. "Belligerent," he said. "Good word 'belligerent.' I like that."

"Please, sir. I am only trying to protect the interests of our passengers here."

"Of course you are. And I assume this boat line likes to cooperate with the law. Is that right?"

"Absolutely, sir. We have the utmost respect for law and order. Always."

"Yeah, I kinda thought you would. So I tell you what. You boys can do me a favor and save me some bother if

25

you put this piece of walking slime in leg irons and lock him away somewhere till we get to St. Louie. I'll take him off your hands and turn him over to the proper authorities there."

"Why, I couldn't do any such thing, sir. You know I could not."

Longarm pulled his wallet out of his coat and opened it to display his badge. "I know you can, mister. I have the authority to arrest this man on charges of interferin' with a federal peace officer . . . that's me, you see . . . in the performance of his duties . . . which is why I happen to be on this boat. Travelin' on official business, don't you see. And this jasper interfered with me. Which happens to be a crime. He threatened my person. That's a crime, too. And he interfered with the constitutional rights of another party, which hasn't been mentioned here so far. And that is also a crime. So y'see, I can see to it that this asshole spends the next three, four years in prison. Or I might just decide to beat the shit outa him and throw him overboard and be done with it. But what I am *not* gonna do is take any crap. Not offa him. Not offa you. Are we clear on this?" Longarm stood. He was at least six inches taller than the shipping line officer. He glared across the man's head toward the passenger, who all of a sudden had a rather sickly expression.

"I . . . I . . . You're just hiding behind that badge. You aren't man enough to do anything without it. I know your kind. Without that badge and that big gun you're nothing. Take them off and I'll whip your ass, mister."

Belligerent, Longarm thought. Yup. That word did seem to cover things.

"D'you want to have it out man-to-man then, just the two of us up on the sun deck? D'you really want to face me? No badge, no gun, nothing like that. Just the two of us and we're quits afterward without no complaints to the company or charges filed? D'you really want to do that? Or do you always hafta have somebody else do the hard part for you?"

There was not a sound in the dining room, not the clink of a fork on china or the rattle of a cup in a saucer, while the other passengers waited to hear what the big man's response would be.

Chapter 7

The passenger sneered and tried to spit in Longarm's face. He did not do a very good job of it—which was probably very fortunate for him—because the stream of sputum landed in the ship's officer's hair and brought an exclamation of considerable disgust from that fellow. Longarm judged that this passenger was not going to be popular on board the *Sacagawea* no matter what else happened.

"All right," he said. "Upstairs." Longarm turned and strode outside and looked for the ladder that would take them to the topmost deck, where the passengers could sit in lounge chairs to watch the passing scenery. There was a fairly large open area, perhaps ten feet by thirty, behind the smokestacks, which he suddenly recalled were termed "chimneys" by the riverboaters.

The officer followed Longarm while the blustery and now thoroughly enraged passenger hung several paces behind. And behind him were a good two thirds of the men who had been in the dining salon.

Longarm kept a wary eye on his opponent while he stripped off his coat and gunbelt and handed them to a waiter who had come up with everyone else. "Don't let

nothing happen to the cheroots I got in my pocket there."
He winked at the waiter and got a laugh in return.

Meanwhile the passenger was stripping to the waist. He
was a prick, but he was not a soft one, Longarm saw. The
man had good muscle and size. The question was whether
he had heart. Longarm very much doubted that he did.

"This is going to be a fair fight," the ship's officer announced in a loud voice. "The loser will be required to go
ashore at our next landing. I want you both to be clear on
that. We cannot condone these disruptions." Despite that
statement, he did not sound at all unhappy about the idea of
two passengers engaging in a brawl on board, and if anything, he seemed rather pleased. But then he was still
scrubbing the top of his head with a linen napkin, trying to
remove the spit from his hair.

"Get outa the damn way," the passenger snarled.

"Please, Mr. Gardner, I want—"

The passenger, Gardner, ignored the officer and rushed
Longarm, who was patiently standing and waiting.

Longarm let him come, then slipped half a step to the
side and let Gardner's bullish charge go by. Longarm could
have hooked a left into Gardner's gut when he passed, but
for the moment he held back, wanting a little time to size
up his opponent.

Gardner stopped short and, instead of spinning around
to face Longarm, lashed out in a cowkick back and to the
side, the heel of his shoe aiming for Longarm's left knee.
If the kick had landed—and it damn near did—it would
have been a disabling blow, but Longarm slid out of reach
in time to avoid injury. It seemed that Gardner was a tricky
son of a bitch, though. That kick had been unexpected.

"I said to fight fair," the ship's officer yelped. "No kicking. No gouging neither."

"Get fucked," Gardner snarled.

Longarm's lips thinned just a little. But the expression
was far from being a smile. It was an acknowledgment.

30

There were indeed rules in this scrap. Gardner had just set them. So be it.

Gardner raised his fists in a classic boxer's pose and hunched his shoulders, then shuffled cautiously forward, knowing now that Longarm was not likely to be overwhelmed by a bullrush.

"Are you going to fight, lawman, or will you just stand there?" he taunted.

"In a hurry, are you?"

Gardner leaned in and probed with a left, then followed that with a sharp right hand.

Longarm swayed out of the way of the serious punch and stepped in behind it to rip a right of his own into the man's belly.

Gardner grunted and backpedaled quickly out of reach, Longarm following.

Gardner popped two, three, four left jabs toward Longarm's jaw then again tried that powerful right.

Longarm caught the right on his forearm and flicked it away, then drove his own right fist into Gardner's face. The big man staggered backward, windmilling his arms and looking quite startled when he found himself on his butt in the center of a crowd of laughing, hooting passengers.

He bounced to his feet and yelled, "He tripped me. You saw it. He tripped me."

"Come on then," Longarm responded. "I'll trip you again just like that time."

Gardner lowered his head and again came on in a rush. Longarm sidestepped and this time did slam a left into his gut, turned and stepped forward to deliver a right that missed Gardner's jaw and landed on the man's ear. A trickle of blood began to flow onto his neck.

Gardner stood for a moment, head down and chest heaving. He had the muscle but was becoming winded awfully easily, Longarm thought. This was not going to last very long now. Not if Gardner was already wearing out.

Gardner took several deep breaths and seemed to collect himself, then turned and tried again, shuffling forward but flat-footed now and not on the balls of his feet. Moving like that, he did not have good balance. Longarm stopped him with a sharp jab flush on the cheekbone, then sent a right wrist deep into Gardner's belly.

"Foul. He fouled me," Gardner screamed, bending over.

"Not yet," Longarm said.

And kicked the son of a bitch in the knee.

Gardner dropped like a two-hundred-pound sack of grain. He hit the deck with a loud thump.

"There. Now I've fouled you," Longarm said rather mildly. He was dimly aware that the promenade was crowded now and people were screaming. Someone seemed to be taking bets on the outcome of the fight.

Gardner came shakily to his feet. He was bleeding from the ear, and the skin was split and bleeding heavily over his right cheekbone. The extent of Longarm's damage was that his shirttail was beginning to pull out of his trousers.

"You bastard," Gardner rasped. "Damn you to hell."

"Let it be, mister. You've been whipped. There's no cause to make it any worse. Let it be."

"Nobody . . . nobody does this to me and gets away with it."

"Mister, I just did. Now, turn around and go away."

Gardner bent over, hands braced on his knees while he sucked air for a moment. Then he straightened and stepped forward with his hand extended to shake.

"Fair enough," Longarm said. He offered his own hand.

Gardner's left hand flashed and Longarm heard the ugly snick of a spring-loaded knife snapping open, the suddenly exposed blade slashing toward his belly.

Longarm jumped backward. He felt the passage of the blade over the rough cloth of his vest but had no time to determine if he had been cut. He chopped down hard with the edge of his hand, the blow landing on Gardner's wrist.

32

He heard the snap of breaking bone. A scream. A clatter as the knife fell onto the deck. Gardner dropped to his knees in pain.

"Here," Longarm said. "Let me help you up." He took Gardner's hand and pulled the big man to his feet. Gardner screamed again and went instantly pale. His eyes rolled back in his head and he dropped flat onto the deck, passed out cold.

"Oh, my," Longarm said. "Is that the arm that's busted? Tsk tsk. My mistake. You prick."

He turned and looked for the waiter, who had his coat. He wanted a smoke now. And maybe a shot of good rye whiskey to go with it.

Gardner was still sprawled out unconscious when Longarm pressed through the crowd and made his way to the stairs—ladder, dammit—down to the salon.

Chapter 8

The *Sacagawea*'s steam whistle shrilled, the sound of it piercing the late afternoon air and sending a flock of small birds fluttering like a brown cloud out of a copse of trees just upriver from the landing.

Junius Gardner, his forearm in a splint wrapped tight with linen, stood beside his luggage on shore while the big paddles of the sternwheeler began to churn backward, pulling the boat slowly away from the quay.

Gardner's mouth moved, but Longarm, standing on the promenade, could not hear his words over the noise of the paddles and the scream of the whistle. He did see the shape of the man's lips and thought he was saying something about a son of somebody's female dog. But he did not know who Gardner could possibly mean by that. Longarm smiled and gave the asshole a cheery wave goodbye.

The first mate had said the loser would be put off the boat, and so he had been. Without a refund of his fare, Longarm understood. Bastard.

Gardner shouted something else, that sound, too, swallowed up by the surrounding noise and the rapidly increasing distance between them, and Longarm grinned and waved to him again. Gardner did not wave back.

The *Sacagawea* reached the channel and the whistle shrieked again. The boat slowed and the paddles reversed themselves and began once more to churn, driving the boat forward, the bow swinging to join with the current and again head downstream toward distant St. Louis and points beyond.

Longarm heard a faint titter of contained laughter behind him and turned. Immediately he swept his hat off and inclined his head in the lady's direction. "Good afternoon, miss."

"Good afternoon, sir. Excuse me, please. I don't mean to make light of this. But I thought it quite amusing when you waved goodbye to him."

Longarm grinned and shrugged.

"Are you really a deputy marshal, sir?"

"Forgive me for forgettin' my manners, miss." Longarm introduced himself to the angelic creature he'd so admired back in Omaha and again at breakfast this morning.

"My name is Eloise Stephens, Marshal."

"Pleased to meet you, Miss Stephens."

"Oh dear, that sounds so dreadfully formal, doesn't it. Please call he Wheezy." Her smile would melt granite. "All my friends do."

"Wheezy?"

She laughed. "Really."

"Somehow that doesn't seem to fit you, but if that's what you want . . ."

"What do your friends call you, Deputy Marshal Long?"

"Apart from a lot of names that oughtn't to be spoken in the presence of a lady, they mostly call me Longarm. Has to do with the long arm of the law, you see." There were other possible explanations, too, but he certainly did not want to bring any of that up with an innocent young girl.

"Then I shall call you that, too, Longarm." She took a

few steps forward, so that she was standing close beside him, leaning on the railing and peering out at the riverbank, which was again beginning to slide past them. The river surface was quiet, and Longarm had the impression, false but nonetheless strong, that it was the *Sacagawea* that was motionless and the riverbank that was flowing by.

"May I confess something to you, Longarm?"

He smiled. "Confess? I can't believe a girl like you would be guilty of crimes in need of confessing."

Wheezy laughed. "Not that sort of confession. It is that . . . Oh, I do hope you will not think ill of me when I tell you this . . . but I sneaked onto the sun deck this morning. I was watching when you and that man . . . It was . . . You were . . . quite . . . You will think me bold, I know."

Longarm waited for her to go on, and after a moment she said, "You were magnificent, Longarm. Strong and quick. You reminded me of some great jungle cat. I've never seen a tiger. Not in real life. But this morning your movements were what I imagine a tiger's would have been. It was . . . oh, dear . . . I am far too bold . . . but the truth is, to watch you like that was quite . . . thrilling. Really. I became . . ." She turned and peered up at him from close range, her eyes—a bright and startling blue—huge pools that mesmerized and beckoned him. In a throaty whisper she said, "I was aroused, Longarm." She very lightly touched his wrist. "You made me get all wet."

It was a damned good thing Longarm smoked rather than chewed, because if he'd had a chew of tobacco in his mouth at that moment, he would have swallowed it for sure.

"Oh, dear. I've offended you. Please forgive me."

And with that Eloise Stephens turned and hurried away, leaving a very perplexed Longarm standing at the rail. With a hard-on bulging the buttons at his fly.

Jesus H. Christ, he thought.

Wheezy couldn't be well into her teens yet, and she was

talking like that about things that she shouldn't even understand at that age.

But . . . the plain truth was that it wasn't fatherly or protective that he was feeling about her right now.

If she were just a little older . . . or he a little younger . . .

Chapter 9

"Shall we reconvene after dinner then, gentlemen?" Longarm asked the gents seated around the card table. A steward had just announced dinner, and several of the men were anxious to eat.

Longarm assembled his coins into a loose pile, then cupped his hand beneath the edge of the table and swept them onto his palm before dropping them uncounted into a pocket.

"Coming, Long?" Hirt asked.

"I'll be along in a minute," he answered, then with a grin added, "Want to go down to my cabin and sniff my armpit to see if I need a fresh shirt before we dine."

The others laughed and turned toward the bow while Longarm headed onto the outside walkway and down to the main deck. He took his time, in no hurry to join the rush. Let others do that. It would be another full day before they reached St. Louis, and he could eat at any time.

When he reached number 11, though, he came to a frowning halt. The transom over the door was propped slightly open. And he distinctly remembered closing it before he went up to play cards.

Longarm pressed his back to the wall and drew his Colt

Thunderer, holding it up at a sharp angle while he reached over and with his left hand very slowly, very quietly turned the doorknob until the latch came free.

Then, taking a deep breath, he shoved the door open with a bang and, shouting to distract anyone who might be lurking inside, charged into the tiny cabin.

He was not two paces into the cabin before he drew up short, his eyes wide in utter astonishment at the sight of what was waiting for him in there.

Chapter 10

Eloise Stephens had tits. His knowledge about that was not academic, was not of the "every girl does" variety; he knew damn good and well that she did. He could see them.

The girl was sprawled on her back on Longarm's bunk, and she was as naked as the day she was born.

"My god, girl, cover yourself."

She laughed.

"Please. What the hell would people think." And, reminded of that, he quickly took half a step back and shut the cabin door. Not that anyone was apt to wander past all the way back here at the ass end of the boat, but you never knew.

And sometimes the most unlikely of consequences can occur at the most embarrassing of moments. There seemed to be some sort of unwritten rule about that.

"My question," the girl said, "is whether you are going to shoot me with that thing in your hand."

Longarm blinked. Then realized what it was she was talking about. He was still holding his revolver ready to shoot an intruder. Except . . .

He hastily slid the Colt back into his holster.

"There is something sexy about guns, don't you think?"

41

"No, I damn well do *not* think. What the hell's the matter with you, child?"

Eloise laughed again. "Child? Just how old do you think I am, Marshal Custis Longarm Long?"

"Shit, I dunno. Fourteen? Fifteen maybe? Somewhere along about there."

That brought a huge laugh out of her. "You idiot. I am twenty-three years old. Did you think I was some simpering little virgin or something? Longarm dear, I haven't been that since I was twelve years old and asked the boy next door what his dog and mine were doing. He showed me, dear. And I discovered a wonderful new toy. Now tell me something. Why are we wasting all this time talking when we could be fucking instead?"

"You can't be twenty-three. I'd easier believe you was twelve than twenty-three."

"Do you want me to take you home and get the priest to show you my baptismal record?"

"No, but . . ."

"Longarm, dear . . ." She came sinuously off the bunk, gloriously naked and slim and smooth, her waist tiny, thighs sleek and small, belly flat, pubic hair so sparse he wondered if she plucked it, and those tits. Her tits were small, perfectly formed little cones with little pink tips on them. The old saying about more than a mouthful came to mind when he looked at her. There was nothing on Eloise that was wasted.

But what was there was prime.

"I . . . Oh, shit."

She wrapped herself around him, supple as a snake and clinging just as close as one, tight to him. She raised her mouth to his while one hand crept between his belly and hers to begin unfastening the buttons at his fly. She acted like this was something she knew how to do. Might even have done it before a time or two.

"You were saying something?" she whispered into his

mouth. Her breath was sweet. It tasted of something mighty pleasant. Mint, he thought.

"Hush," he told her.

He picked her up—she weighed next to nothing—and she laughed when he bumped her feet into the wall in the close confinement of the steamboat cabin. Longarm deposited her lightly onto the bunk, and Eloise reached up to complete her self-appointed task of getting his cock out of his trousers.

That was easier for her now that she was down below his belt level, and she quickly got down to what she wanted. The girl's eyes widened with surprise and she burst into a huge smile when she saw the size of what she found there.

"Beautiful," she exclaimed. She leaned forward, holding his erection in both hands, and placed the softness of her cheek against his shaft as if hugging him, then ran the tip of her nose up and down the length of him.

She looked up and giggled with delight. "You are such a beautiful man."

"Keep on talkin'," he said. "I can feel your breath all warm and nice on me there when you do."

"Oh, I can do better than that, dear." She began to lick his cock, lifted his balls and gave them a slow and thorough licking, too, then went back to nibbling his cock as if it were an ear of early corn.

"Jesus!" Longarm exclaimed. His legs felt weak and he braced himself with one hand against the wall when Eloise peeled back his foreskin and ran her tongue around and around the head of his cock.

She giggled again and took him into her mouth, the wet heat of her driving him half-mad.

Abruptly she pulled back. "Don't you dare finish in my mouth. I like the taste of a man just fine, but I don't want to waste this before I have a chance to feel it inside me."

"I wouldn't think of it," he lied. He would not only think of it, he'd quite happily spill a quart of it down this girl's throat if she gave him half a chance. And time enough to work up that much jism.

Eloise sucked on him for another minute or so, then tugged him down onto her.

"Look, uh, don't you want me to take off these clothes?"

"No, please don't. I want to feel that gun of yours against my stomach."

"Which gun?"

"I agree they both seem like steel, but I was talking about the blue one. I want the pink one inside me, thank you." She looked at it again. "I've never felt anything that big before."

"If you think I'd hurt you . . ."

"Will you please shut up! I am not complaining; I'm anticipating. Now, bring it here, will you." She lay back on the narrow bunk and spread her legs wide.

The left leg, he noticed, did not bend, which would account for the awkward gait. Or rather it seemed to be permanently very slightly bent at the knee, and that would effectively make it shorter than the right even if they were the exact same length when her right leg was bent also. It was a handicap that did not slow Eloise down any, and it damn sure did not detract from the girl's beauty. Lordy, but she was one pretty little thing.

The girl lifted her hips to accommodate his entry, and Longarm slid deep inside her body.

After that . . . Shit, it was like she exploded.

Longarm had ridden down unbroken horses that couldn't buck as hard or as violently as Eloise Stephens. The girl just plain went crazy. Grabbing hold of him with both arms and her right leg, scratching his back, her heel pressed hard against his ass to nail him in place while she tried to split herself in two using his cock for a chisel. She even hung on with her teeth, so that he was glad he still had his clothes on. She locked her teeth tight in his coat at the shoulder and hung on to him there, too. He was convinced

44

she would've taken a chunk out of him if she'd had meat clamped in her jaws instead of tweed. And while she was doing that she was snuffling and grunting like a half-grown pig that was cheek deep in the trough.

The girl with a cock inside her was a wild thing, only half-human and the other half something else entirely.

Not that he was complaining. He'd heard the expression "fuck your brains out," and he was now convinced that such a thing was possible. Eloise Stephens could do it if anybody ever could.

She leaped and clung, whinnied and tossed her head back and forth, gasped and grunted. And all the while that pretty little ass was churning away fit to grind coffee if he'd only thought to throw a handful of beans between their bellies.

The truth, though, was that he was not exactly sure just how much he liked this treatment. It sounded fine in the abstract, a wild and woolly ride like that atop a beautiful young woman, but in practice he found himself wondering if a big candle wouldn't have done just as much for her as his pecker did. Longarm himself seemed to have gotten lost along the way somewhere.

She could damn sure pull the juice out of a man, though. He came quickly, built up and came again a few minutes later, and was working up to a third explosion of his own when Eloise turned loose of his coat and threw her head back, her slim and seemingly delicate neck corded, the veins standing out against the surface of her skin.

She went entirely rigid, a loud, keening squeal rising behind her tightly clenched teeth.

And then she collapsed. Passed out cold and completely limp as her own climax overtook and exhausted her.

Jesus, Longarm thought.

With Eloise lying inert beneath him, he stroked gently in and out for a moment to finish that third outburst and then withdrew.

He had quite forgotten the Colt revolver, but now he could see the faint darkening that would be the beginnings of a bruise on her belly. Her flesh was very pale and looked tender.

Longarm shuddered once and stood. He found the scrap of soft washcloth that had come with the towel in his cabin and used that to wipe himself, then put things away and buttoned up again.

Eloise was still passed out. And all of a sudden he realized where the girl got her nickname. She had so utterly exhausted herself fucking that her breath was ragged and she was, well, wheezing.

Wheezy indeed, he thought. It made perfect sense to him now.

Longarm sat on the foot of the bunk and took out a cheroot to smoke while he waited for Wheezy to come around.

He was not entirely sure at that moment if he wanted to crawl into the middle of this girl a second time or . . .

He looked at her body, lying naked and beautiful, and, aw, hell. Any girl that pretty deserved a second chance.

Chapter 11

Once she got up and dressed, Longarm was about half-convinced nothing had happened. To look at the girl, you wouldn't think she ever had to take a crap like an ordinary human person. Porcelain figurines don't shit, do they? Surely Wheezy Stephens didn't either. Or if she did, then at the very least it didn't stink. Why, the very thought of this girl with a dick in her mouth . . . Impossible, of course. He'd obviously imagined the whole thing. Delirium, that's what it was.

"Tomorrow morning," the girl said as she finished tidying her hair into place. "We must do this again tomorrow morning, while there is still time."

"Still time?" Longarm asked.

Wheezy stood up and smoothed down the fabric of her gown.

"I shall be leaving the boat in St. Louis and traveling up the Mississippi on a different craft," she said.

Longarm grunted. "As it happens, so will I."

Wheezy gave him a speculative look. "The nice man at the Grant arranged my passage on a boat called the *Willis Adams*."

47

"Uh-huh. Same fella made my booking. Same boat, too."

"My," she said, picking up her handbag with an enigmatic smile. "How very convenient." And then she was gone, whisking away before he had a chance to open the door or so much as tell her a swift goodbye.

She was some girl that Wheezy Stephens.

And awfully well named.

Longarm scouted up his coat and fished around inside it for a cheroot. He felt like he needed a good smoke to help him recover. A smoke and a stiff shot of rye whiskey. Maybe several.

Propriety was one thing, spendthrift extravagance another. Since they were going to the same place anyway, Longarm and the girl shared a cab when they left the *Sacagawea* for the *Willis Adams*. The distance between their quays was less than a quarter mile, but Wheezy was not one to travel light. She was accompanied by half a dozen bags and boxes of luggage. And Longarm, gentleman though he was, was not about to carry all that shit for her. Better to pay for the cab. Better yet, let the government pay for the cab. The United States Treasury could likely afford it.

When they got to the designated place, Longarm frowned when he climbed out of the hansom and stared at an empty berth where the *Willis Adams* should have been.

"Are you sure this is where we're supposed to be?" he asked the driver.

The man's silent response was to tilt his whip toward a sign beside the quay.

"Albermarle Packet Line and Shipping Co. Operating river and coastal steamers *Edmund Adams, Cremona Adams, Willis Adams* and *Fedenda*. Passenger, freight and transshipment services at reasonable rates. Inquire within."

The sign was posted over an arch that once was painted white but now was weathered gray. Just inside the arch on the quayside was a small shack that presumably served as the line's St. Louis ticket office.

"Wait here," Longarm told Wheezy. "I'll go ask about the boat." He held a finger up to caution the hansom driver about discharging his fare too quickly, then strode through the arch to the ticket office.

A group of half a dozen or so muscular blacks were loafing in the shade beside the office, seated on some bales of freight awaiting loading onto a boat that was not there. Inside there was a gray-haired man with a truly magnificent steel-gray mustache. He sat behind a desk, feet propped up and a newspaper laid open in his lap.

"Afternoon," Longarm said. "Me and another passenger off the *Sacagawea* are supposed to board the *Willis Adams* this afternoon."

"Well, it isn't here," the agent said without looking up from his newspaper.

"I can see that for myself, mister. Isn't it supposed to be here now?"

"Yep. Supposed to. Isn't."

"Would you mind telling me when it will be here?"

The man folded his paper and laid it aside, finally dropping his heels off the desk and looking at Longarm. "Mister, the *Willis,* she's hung up on a sandbar about a hundred fifty miles south of here. Damn fool pilot tried to cut a corner when they were racing some other boat is what the captain said in his wire. Must've drove hard onto that bar to get hung up this bad, and likely there's things the captain isn't telling, not over a wire that could be read by just anybody. Point is, I'm not exactly sure when the *Willis* is gonna get here. Tomorrow morning would be the earliest you could look for her, and God knows when she'll actually pull in. If you'll give me your name and . . . You said there's another passenger waiting for her, too?"

"I did. A young lady."

"Well, give me your names and the name of the hotel

49

where you'll be. As soon as I receive a good arrival time for the *Willis*, I'll send a boy to tell you when you can expect her."

"That sounds fair enough. Let me go see if the young lady has a preference about where to stay. I'll be right back."

Chapter 12

Wheezy gave Longarm a worried look, then glanced at the hansom driver. "We need to talk," she whispered.

He raised an eyebrow.

"In private."

"All right." To the cabbie he said, "Wait here. We'll be going on to a hotel in a few minutes."

"Whatever you say, mister. Just mind you that you'll be paying for my time."

Longarm ignored that and helped Wheezy down from the cab, then led her out onto the empty quay far enough that none of the stevedores could overhear. He checked behind the stacks of freight waiting to be loaded, then asked her, "What's the mystery?"

"I find . . ." She hesitated and dropped her eyes away from his. "This is difficult for me to say."

"Take your time." He reached into his coat for a cheroot and busied himself with lighting it.

Still in a low whisper the girl said, "I find that I am . . . how shall I put this . . . financially embarrassed." Tears began to leak from her eyes and roll unchecked across those soft and perfect cheeks.

"You're busted," he said.

She ran the back of her hand over her eyes to dry the tears. "In a word, yes. I shall not bore you with all the silly details, but . . . yes. I am far from home. I have no money. And now I face disgrace on top of all that. Please, Custis. Please help me. And, Custis. Please keep my secret. I am not the sort of girl who . . ." She began to blush. But then Custis Long knew what sort of girl she really was.

"What d'you want me to do, Wheezy?"

"Could you possibly . . . My ticket is all paid for, you see. I spent the very last of my meager funds to secure that before . . ." She did not finish the sentence but took a deep, shuddering breath. "I did not anticipate this layover in St. Louis. I have no money for a hotel room, dear. Could we . . . Would it be possible . . . when we get to the hotel . . . ?"

"You mean like pretend we're married or something like that?"

"We wouldn't have to actually say anything. I mean, I would not ask you to actually lie on my behalf. But if we were to simply act like, well like newlyweds . . ."

Longarm exhaled a stream of pale smoke through a crooked grin. "The way I remember it, Wheezy, we kinda been acting like newly married."

The girl managed a smile. "Are you complaining, sir?"

"Not hardly."

"Would you mind so terribly? A little more, um . . ." Her gaze dropped to Longarm's fly, the portal to all the good fun and fine feelings that lay within. Her voice dropped again to a throaty whisper. "I could stand it if you can, dear."

"All right. I reckon it won't hurt nothing."

Wheezy smiled. Her shoulders straightened and she regained her normal confidence instantly. "I knew you were a gentleman, Custis. The very moment I saw you, I knew it. Thank you, dear. Thank you ever so much. What hotel will we be going to?" Without waiting for an answer, she said,

"Could we stay at the Fairview? It is my favorite, you see. I think you will like it. Would that be all right?" The tone of her voice left no room for objection. Of course it would be the Fairview. After all, it was her favorite. What other choice could there possibly be?

And indeed there could be none. Longarm had had his chance to let Wheezy go her own way. That moment was gone now.

He took another long pull on the cheroot. There were, he admitted, worse things that could happen to a man than being trapped in the company of a high-powered fucking machine like Eloise Stephens.

"Let me take you back to the cab," he said, offering his elbow. "Then I'll go in and tell the steamboat agent he can find us at this Fairview Hotel."

"Thank you. Oh, thank you, dear Custis." There was a bright sparkle in her eye when she added, "I shall try ever so hard to make sure you do not regret helping me." She laughed. "If you take my meaning, dear."

She clung tight to his arm as they walked back to the waiting hansom.

Chapter 13

A trickle of sweat collected on Wheezy's forehead, ran down into her eyes and continued past her nose, dripped onto her lower lip and rolled down to the point of her chin. Droplets collected there, then fell with a warm splat onto Longarm's chest.

It was hot inside their airless hotel room. They could not possibly open the window. Not until Wheezy was done riding him, they couldn't. If they did, the whole neighborhood, hell maybe all of St. Louis, was bound to hear Wheezy's grunting and huffing and wheezing. To say nothing of the creak of the bedsprings and the thump of the headboard banging against the wall.

Longarm hoped there was nobody in the next room trying to take an afternoon nap, because this much racket would make sleep impossible. Would likely make them horny as hell, too, of course.

The first thing Wheezy had done after they checked in was take her clothes off. The second was to remove Longarm's clothes. And the third was to drop to her knees and begin sucking his cock.

He'd already come twice, once in her mouth and the next time on top of her. Now he was lying on his back with his erection pointing skyward, while Wheezy rode him like a bucking bronco. Except she was the one doing the bucking. Lordy, but that girl did go into a frenzy when she had a dick to play with.

Longarm lay there admiring the girl's scrawny, sweaty body while she swiveled and pumped, hips grinding and eyes closed.

Wheezy's tits were so small and firm that they scarcely bounced even with all this jumping up and down. She could not bend the bad leg, of course, but she managed nicely enough anyway, extending it beside Longarm's shoulder and squatting with her good leg. The odd position gave her a sort of sideways roll and wiggle to her pumping. Felt mighty good, too, he judged. Big as he was—and he was—Wheezy had no trouble at all taking all of him into that small and seemingly fragile body.

Fragile? Harness leather was less strong, durable and supple.

"Custis. I'm co . . . co . . . coming!"

The girl screamed—there was no other way to put it; never mind their surroundings, she just reared back and roared—then her eyes rolled back in her head and she collapsed, falling backward onto Longarm's legs in a dead faint.

His pecker popped out of its socket and stood rigidly upright. Wheezy might have made it that time, but he hadn't.

Not that he was concerned. After getting off twice already, he could wait a little longer for the third explosion.

He sighed and wriggled out from under Wheezy's inert form, then sat up on the side of the bed to reach for a cigar and his matches. His hard-on slowly subsided, until the blind snake was pointing toward the floor rather than the ceiling.

A glance at Wheezy assured him that she was still alive

and breathing. There was really nothing he could do for her now, and he'd already learned not to worry about it.

She was an odd little girl, though, this Wheezy Stephens.

He wondered if she really could produce a baptismal certificate to show she was of age.

Then he smiled. Yeah, probably she could. And if one didn't exist already, she would probably up and seduce some poor priest so she could get him to forge the documents she wanted. Longarm had an idea that little Wheezy most generally managed to get what she wanted.

He bit the twist off the end of his cheroot and spat the fleck of tobacco into his palm, then scraped a match along the headboard to set it afire so he could light his smoke.

The tobacco tasted fine. A drink would be even better.

He had a pint of rye in his bag but . . . dammit, he wanted some air as much as he did the whiskey.

Come to think of it . . .

He got up and padded naked and barefoot over to the window, unlatched it and tugged it open to allow a faint puff of warm breeze to enter. The clip-clop sounds of traffic passing on the street below and a few voices from passersby entered the hotel room along with the fresh air.

The sweat of his chest—his own and a fair amount of Wheezy's sweat, too—felt chill when the air reached it. It felt good.

Wheezy would be out cold for another five or ten minutes, he judged, deciding he did not want to wait around for her to wake up.

The Fairview—rather badly named since there was damned little view and none of that particularly fair—provided guests with a tiny desk, pencils and some pieces of mismatched paper. Longarm chose a small slip of paper and quickly jotted a note for the girl. He could leave it propped on the mirror, he thought. She was sure to see it there as soon as she woke.

"Couldn't sleep. Gone downstairs for a drink. Join me there for supper." He signed it with a large L and replaced the pencil in the cup of them the hotel provided, then carried his note to the dressing table.

He dressed quickly and let himself out into the hallway.

Wheezy still lay in an exhausted, sweat-drenched stupor on the hotel's lumpy bed.

Fine girl, that Wheezy, Longarm thought as he made his way downstairs. Cute. Damned pity she was so shy, though.

Chapter 14

"Custis," Wheezy said as he escorted her away from the table, she seeming to glow with vibrant health and he marveling that any creature, even a bird, might be able to survive on so little in the way of food. Of course what she lacked in normal food she certainly made up for by eating cock and swallowing jism. She was one helluva girl, this Wheezy Stephens.

"Yes?" he said, offering his elbow and undoubtedly creating a maelstrom of envy throughout the dining room.

"Might I ask a huge, *huge* favor of you?" Her eyes were bigger than any favor she could possibly ask. Big and wide open and innocent.

"You can always ask. Remains to be seen if it's for something I can give, though."

Wheezy smiled. "I don't believe this should be so very difficult. You see, dear, there are some things that a girl . . . well . . . does not want to share. There are some moments that really should be private."

Which seemed a very strange statement from a girl who just a couple hours earlier was flat on her back licking his asshole.

"Would you be a dear, dear, and have them send a tub

and hot water to the room. Then, well, would you disappear for a few hours, please? Go shopping or whatever it is men do."

Longarm tipped his head back and laughed.

"Did I say something funny, dear?"

"No, darlin', not at all. Two, three hours be enough time?"

"Oh, three hours would be perfect." Her eyes became even larger and more luminous, something he would not have thought possible had he not seen it, and she very lightly laid her fingertips on his wrist. "I would be happy to, shall we say . . . *reward* you, Custis. When you get back."

"Now you've stuck me right in the middle of one of them whachamacallits. A dilemma."

"How is that, dear?"

"I'm wantin' to stay out even longer to make you all the more grateful, but at the same time I'm not wantin' to leave to begin with, so's I can collect on that reward you mentioned."

It was Wheezy's turn to laugh. Then, very slowly mounting the stairs to accommodate her shortened leg, she said, "The reward is already yours to claim, dear, so if you want it now instead of . . ."

"No, I was just funning you, Wheezy. You go ahead and do the girl things that you figure need doin'. I can always find a card game or a billiards table. You shall have your three hours, girl." He winked at her. "But don't count on no longer'n that."

Wheezy gave him a knowing smile and continued on up the steps at her rather awkward pace.

Longarm saw her to their room and opened it for her but stopped at the threshold. "Now, mind you bolt this door behind me. I'll have your tub an' water sent up, but as soon as the boys is gone from delivering them you bolt the door

60

again. I wouldn't want nothing to happen to you." He grinned and added, "Not until I get back, that is."

Wheezy giggled.

"Promise me."

She became sober for a moment. "All right. I promise. Can I have a kiss to seal the bargain?"

"You ask a helluva lot but . . . all right." He swept her up in a bear hug and did his level best to lick her tonsils. Thought he damn near got down to them, too.

When he released her, Wheezy was gasping. "Oh, my," she whispered. "I don't know if I can let you go after that. Are you sure you have to be gone three whole hours, dear? Perhaps you could return a little sooner. You have made me quite wet again from wanting you."

"Three hours," Longarm said, pulling his watch out and checking the time. "Look for me to come knocking not a minute past that time."

Wheezy kissed him again and slipped inside the hotel room, closing the door behind her.

Longarm waited until he heard the bolt slide closed before he turned away and went downstairs to order the tub and bathwater. And to find some way to kill three hours.

Kill time, hell. What he needed was to find a quick way to recuperate, because after those three hours were up . . .

Chapter 15

The best way Longarm knew to waste a little time in a pleasurable manner—other than a good fuck, which at the moment was out of the question—was with a glass of whiskey, a good cigar and some low-stakes wagering. He took a look inside the so-called "gentlemen's room" in the Fairview and quickly decided this was not the place.

The Fairview's salon—spelled with one "o," thank you very much—was tiny, dark and nearly empty. Two old codgers were playing a desultory game of cribbage while a third sat snoring with his beard pushing on his chest. There was likely a bartender somewhere in the building, but Longarm could not see him. And quickly decided he did not want to. He wanted a saloon not a salon, and one with a little life to it. It was either that or wake the sleeping graybeard and invite him to a rousing game of cribbage. Longarm decided to look elsewhere.

He was not familiar with this part of St. Louis, but all cities are pretty much alike in some respects, opportunities for indulgence in the vices being chief among them. He went outside, tossed a mental coin as to which way to turn and wheeled to his right.

He made a bet with himself that he would be able to

find a suitable saloon within three blocks at the most. And, funny thing, he won. There was a noisy, happy, very slightly rowdy workingman's sort of place the next block over. Longarm ambled inside and felt very much at home.

"What'll you have, mister?" the barman said in greeting, having to raise his voice to be heard over the buzz of several dozen conversations.

"Do you have rye whiskey?" Longarm knew better than to get picky about label or origin in a place like this one.

"Does a chicken have lips?" the barman asked.

"No, but it has a pecker," Longarm finished the old chestnut for him.

The bartender's lips thinned in what might have been an attempt at a smile. "Yeah, and we got rye," he said.

"A glass then, not a shot."

"You want a chaser with that?"

Longarm shook his head. He fished in his pocket for the handful of small change he'd been using to play cards with back on the steamboat and paid for his drink. Somehow he didn't think it would be prudent to be dragging out the gold coins or the currency that he also carried. This seemed a nice enough place, but he was among strangers and you just never know.

He took a sip of the rye and nodded. It was all right. Not the very best, but it wasn't horse piss either. He allowed the warmth to spread in his belly and felt refreshed already.

Leaving the whiskey on the bar, he turned halfway around and propped himself on one elbow while he looked the place over. There were several tables with card games in progress.

And two of them looked to be a player or two short.

Longarm picked up the rye and carried it over to the nearer of those tables.

• • •

"I hate to leave when I'm ahead, gents . . . Leastwise that's the sort of thing I'm supposed to say now . . . but I got to go." He stood, leaving a hand of useless cards spread face-down on the table, and scooped up his handful of nickel-and-dime winnings.

"You can't take our money, mister. You can't go now."

Longarm thought at first that the man was joking. But he wasn't, as a closer look at his expression showed.

"It ain't right you should go now. Now set down and stay till this game is over."

"Friend," Longarm said slowly, "for me the game *is* over. That's what I just told you."

"But I'm behind. I can't . . . Shit, man, I can't afford to lose here."

"If you can't afford the loss, there's a simple solution."

"What, mister? Name it."

"Don't play." Longarm dropped the coins into his coat pocket. Lordy, it wasn't like the fellow could have lost all that much. Longarm doubted his winnings totaled more than five dollars, six tops. And this asshole was going to whine about it?

"You got no compassion," the unhappy player accused.

"You're right," Longarm said. "I don't." He turned away, the pleasure of the game ruined now by the whiner.

He went to the bar and counted out his pocketful of coins—$5.25 exactly—and exchanged them for a half ea-gle, the odd quarter going to the bartender as a tip. From the surprised way the bartender responded, Longarm guessed there weren't many tips offered in the place.

"Thank you, mister. You come again now, hear."

Longarm laid a finger against the brim of his Stetson and ambled outside, pausing on the sidewalk to check the time and light a cheroot. He'd been away just over three hours. By now Wheezy should be looking for him.

He could not contain the faint smile that tugged at his lips as he headed back toward the hotel.

Chapter 16

Longarm had not reached the end of the block before he heard someone hurrying along behind him, the footsteps light and rapid. For a moment he thought the person approaching him was the unhappy poker player from back in the saloon. He stopped and turned, only to find that the pedestrian was a woman.

She was shabbily clothed, her dress drab and in need of washing. She had a shawl draped over her shoulders, and her hair was disheveled, flyaway wisps of it coming undone from her bun and giving her an even more unkempt appearance, as did a smudge of something dark—old makeup or simply dirt—on her right cheek.

For some reason she seemed a little nonplussed when Longarm stopped and turned to face her. One hand flew to her throat; the other was plunged deep in a pocket on the side of her dress.

"Oh, I . . . Do you have a light, mister?"

"A light?"

"A match, I mean. Do you have a match?"

"You don't have a cigarette or a cigar or nothing," Longarm pointed out.

"Mister, I asked a simple enough question. I'm wanting

the borrow of a match, that's all. Now, do you have one or don't you?" By then she was standing close in front of him. She was thin, and for a woman she was tall, not more than half a head shorter than he was.

"Sorry," he said. "You're right. It ain't any of my business what you want with one, and I reckon I do have a match that I'd be pleased to give you." He dipped two fingers into his vest pocket to extract the requested lucifer.

While Longarm was occupied with that, the woman's right hand flashed out of her pocket.

He saw the glint of lamplight on steel and jerked backward barely in time to avoid having his throat slashed.

"What the . . . ?"

The woman's first slashing cut missed its mark, but she tried again, reversing the direction of that sweep and striking a backhanded swing at him.

Longarm ducked back away from that one and stepped in close, his left hand clamping tight on the woman's wrist. He bore down. Hard. She squealed and the knife dropped away to clatter harmlessly on the board sidewalk.

"What the hell's the matter with you?" he demanded.

The woman doubled over and bit him on the web of his hand.

"Ouch, dammit." He let go of her wrist, which apparently was what she wanted. "What's this shit all about, lady?"

She might have been a woman, but she was damned sure no lady. She reached down for the knife, but Longarm stopped that by planting his boot on top of the thing, which he could see now was a spring-blade knife, a vicious little fucker even if not usually very sharp or very strong. They were intended for sudden thrusts. For a moment Longarm had a vision of himself staggering into the street with that knife sticking out of his back. If he hadn't turned to see who was following him . . . The thought of it brought a frown to his lips and a shudder throughout his body.

"You," he said, "are under arrest."

"Fuck you," she snarled, coming upright again and scuttling backward.

Longarm expected her to turn and run away into the night. And the plain truth was that would have been just fine with him. He did not know who this crazy woman was or what sort of beef she had—with him or maybe with someone who looked like him from behind, for he could think of no earthly reason why she would want to stab him—but he would have been quite willing to see the last of her. He was tempted to tell her so.

Instead of running, though, she abandoned her pigsticker and stepped backward far enough away that he could not easily grab her. She bent over, eyes locked on Longarm, and lifted the hem of her dress, fumbling beneath it for a moment.

"Hey, dammit!" he barked.

Her hand, when it came into view again, was wrapped around the grips of a small, nickel-plated revolver.

"Now, looka here," he protested. "You can't be doin' this shit now."

The woman did not so much as pause. She cocked the little pistol and fired.

Longarm felt a streak of flame burn the inside of his left arm as a bullet passed between his arm and his ribs. A few inches to one side and he would have had a hole in his lungs at the least and perhaps in his heart.

"Shit," he muttered, watching as the woman, with great determination and steely intent, cocked her little pistol again for another try.

Longarm's Colt roared before he consciously realized that it was in his hand.

The heavy .44 slug impacted on her breastbone, driving her backward several tottering steps before, with a look of puzzled disbelief, she dropped onto her knees.

"Aw, shit," Longarm mumbled. He really hadn't wanted

to do that, dammit. If she'd only given him some choice . . .

The woman was dying and surely knew it, but even so she was not giving up. Her revolver was already cocked. She raised it and took wavering aim in Longarm's direction.

With a sigh of resignation, Longarm fired again, deliberately this time. His bullet put a wet, red mark square in the middle of her forehead . . . and blew half her brains out through the back of her shattered skull.

So much for chivalry, he thought sourly as he quickly shucked the empty casings out of the Colt and replaced those with fresh cartridges from his coat pocket.

By the time Longarm was satisfied there were no other assassins lurking in the shadows, a St. Louis policeman was there, running quickly to the sound of the gunfire. Brave fellow, Longarm thought. He'd known more than a few coppers who liked to wait until all danger was past before they got around to investigating a shooting.

"Put your hands up," the young policeman said. "You are under arrest."

Longarm meekly lifted his hands into the air. The cop was a brave boy, but he was also nervous as hell, and as bad as it would be to be shot on purpose, it would be purely silly to be shot by mistake by a frightened constable.

Chapter 17

"I'm sorry, sir. Really, I . . ." The young cop was babbling apologies now that Longarm had identified himself.

Longarm reached inside his coat and produced his wallet. "Incidentally . . . you said your name is George?"

"Y-yes, sir."

"Something to keep in mind, George. A fella up and tells you he's a deputy U.S. marshal, get him to show his credentials before you take his word for that. A felon could tell you the lie as easy as a deputy tell you the truth, and you could get yourself shot." He flipped the wallet open to display the badge that he very rarely carried in public view.

"Yes, sir. Thank you. Now, Marshal, if you wouldn't mind, sir, would you tell me please what happened here that we have Sarah lying dead on the street?"

"Sarah. I take it you know her?"

"Not personally, but I've seen her around. She, um, works night, you might put it."

"A whore?"

"Well, yes, actually. She is. Was, I mean." George looked down at the dead woman. It was not a pretty sight with all the pink and gray stuff lying in a blob on the sidewalk just behind what was left of Sarah's head.

Longarm explained what had happened, but the young cop shook his head. "That sure as hell doesn't sound like Sarah, Marshal. She's never caused no trouble that I ever heard of. For sure she never hurt nobody."

"Did she work in one of the houses?"

"No, not Sarah. She'd hang out around the saloons. She wouldn't be allowed inside, of course, so she'd stroll out back of the saloons, pick up guys when they'd come out to take a leak. She worked cheap. Lift her skirt right there against a wall or over a empty crate. Get down on her knees and drain the needing out of a fella that way."

The St. Louis policeman picked up Sarah's pistol and her knife, both of them as cheap and shabby as their owner had been, and felt of her pockets. "She was having a good night," he said when he reached into one and extracted a scant handful of coins.

"What d'you mean?"

"Look here. There's a gold double eagle, just as pretty as can be. I've never known Sarah to have more than a couple dollars at one time. Anything more than that she'd go right away down to Chang's place and smoke some opium."

"But not this time," Longarm mused.

"She must've just got her money, otherwise she'd be laying out with a pipe right now."

"I wonder . . . Come to think of it, I may know," Longarm said. "She could have just been paid all right. To plant that knife in my back."

"I don't understand," George said.

"Come with me, Officer. I may need you to arrest somebody."

"What about . . . you know . . . her."

"She ain't going nowhere. My suspect might," Longarm told him.

The cop followed Longarm back to the saloon. There

72

was no sign at the card table of the man who'd been so determined that Longarm not walk away with his winnings.

"Where is the fellow that was in this chair a few minutes ago?" he demanded of the other players.

They glanced first at the policeman, then at Longarm. One of them offered, "He went out to the can. Told us to save his seat, he'd be right back."

"When did he leave?" Longarm asked.

"Right after you went to cash in."

It hadn't taken long for the bartender to count that loose change, Longarm thought. But it might have been time enough for the disgruntled player to spot Sarah and offer her what would have been a huge payday if she would catch up with Longarm and put her knife into his back.

Still . . . twenty dollars . . . perhaps more promised when the job was done . . . and he could not have lost more than a couple dollars. Hell, Longarm's total winnings were barely over five dollars.

Men will do strange things, though, when their pride has been pricked or they think they have been dealt with unjustly. Maybe the guy thought Longarm cheated him.

Or something.

The point now . . .

"Come with me, George. Out back. Let's see if my man really is in the shitter."

They went out the back door and easily found the outhouse. The saloon management very thoughtfully provided a lantern to ease their patrons' path.

Longarm went to the closed door of the shitter and motioned for the cop to stand out of the way. He himself stood well to the side and palmed the big Colt before he pounded on the door.

"Open up," he ordered. "This is the police. You are surrounded. Give yourself up without a fight. Do it *now*!"

73

Chapter 18

"Jesus, God, mister, don't shoot. I ain't carrying a gun. Don't shoot me, please." The man came waddling out of the two-holer with his pants down around his ankles and his hands in the air. Whoever he was, Longarm had never seen this man before in his life and he damn sure was not the unhappy card player who may—or may not—have paid the whore to knife Longarm.

The St. Louis cop pulled out his handcuffs and began to put them on to the frightened saloon patron. Longarm stopped him. "Hold it. That ain't him."

"Then who . . . ?"

"Damn if I know. You! Where's the other fellow?"

"Wh-what other fellow? There's nobody else."

"Was somebody else in there a few minutes ago?"

The man shook his head. "No, nobody. Listen, can I pull my pants up? I don't have a gun or nothing."

"Yeah, I . . . uh . . . I'm sorry. You say no one else has been in there?"

"No, sir. Not while I been here."

"Shit," Longarm said.

Feeling a little better now that he knew he was not the target of the two officers, the innocent fellow ventured, "I

75

already did, mister, and if I hadn't already, I sure would have when you two hollered like you done."

"Yeah, well, I'm sorry about that. Did you see anybody else out back here?"

"Some fella came out just behind me, but he didn't come into the outhouse with me. He turned and went off down the alley."

"Which way?"

The man nodded. Toward the hotel, the direction Longarm had been walking out on the street.

"Do you know a whore named Sarah?"

"There's a couple whores come around here sometimes. I don't know their names."

Longarm described the dead woman for him.

"I've seen her sometimes. What about her?"

"Was she out back here when you came outside to use the shitter?"

The fellow shook his head. "No. Not that I noticed anyway, but then I wasn't looking for no whore. My belly was hurting and I was wanting to get inside there and get my pants down quick as I could. I had to crap awful bad."

"I don't know what to think, George," Longarm admitted to the cop. "There wasn't much time, certainly not enough to set up anything fancy."

"There isn't anything fancy about a knife in the back," the policeman said.

"Oh, God," the innocent townsman said, one hand flying to his throat. "A knife. You don't think . . . ?"

"No, we don't. If we did still think that, you'd be wearing handcuffs right now."

"Thank goodness. Look, I . . . I'm feeling sick. Can I go now?"

"Yeah, go ahead."

The man gave them a worried look and scuttled away down the alley, apparently abandoning any plans to go back inside the saloon to enjoy the rest of the evening.

"Do you want to keep looking for this man you were playing cards with?" George asked.

Longarm considered it. Even if they found him, he would deny having anything to do with the assault. Whether he paid Sarah to kill Longarm or did not, he would swear that he didn't. Barring a confession, there would be no way to prove it either way. Longarm knew better than to expect a voluntary confession. And a confession that is beaten out of a suspect is no more valid than a denial. Either one can be a matter of fear and expediency, having no relationship with the truth.

"No," he answered the cop. "The woman is dead and won't be answering no questions. We'll leave it go at that."

"What about . . . you know."

"I don't reckon I do know what you're asking, George."

"What about Sarah? What should I do with her body?"

"Well if it was up to me," Longarm said, taking out a cheroot, "I expect I'd have her picked up and buried." He snapped a match aflame and lighted his cigar. "But you do whatever you think is right."

Longarm turned and once more headed back toward the hotel, where he was now overdue for that promised rendezvous with Wheezy. He was not, however, feeling particularly randy now, his ardor having been cooled by a whore named Sarah.

Chapter 19

"I was beginning to think you weren't coming back," Wheezy said. There was no hint of pouting in her voice, however, just a simple statement of fact with perhaps a trace of concern. Longarm liked that about her.

"I was delayed," he answered without elaboration. He did not want to upset her.

Wheezy smiled and came to him, her walk provocative even if her clothing was not. She was dressed in a sleeping gown, a very plain and utilitarian garment with no lace or frills. It was almost frumpy. But it was also quite plain that the girl wore nothing beneath it.

"You are here now," she said, wrapping her arms around him and pressing her cheek to his chest. "That is the important thing."

Longarm had been far from horny after the trouble down in the street. But it all came rushing back when Eloise touched him. She disengaged one hand and reached down between their bodies to massage the rapidly growing lump that threatened to burst the buttons at his fly.

The girl looked up at him and smiled again. "One thing I can tell for sure," she said.

"What's that, darlin'?"

"You were not with some other woman." She giggled. "Not and be so hard and ready now."

"No," he said, a momentary image flashing through his mind of Sarah lying dead on the sidewalk with her brains spilling out behind her. "I wasn't with no other woman."

Wheezy looked up at him. "You sound so . . . so serious, dear. Are you all right?"

"Yeah. I'm fine, thanks."

"Even your soldier here is losing interest. Did I say something . . . do something wrong?"

"No, you didn't do nothing wrong," Longarm assured her.

She tried to smile again, but it was only a pale imitation this time. She looked worried. Then, after a moment's hesitation, she brightened, straightening her body and tossing her head to throw a strand of hair out of her eyes. "I'll tell you what," she said. "Let me take your coat and things. You sit right over there in that chair. I had some brandy sent up. We can have a nightcap and relax a little before we . . . do anything. Would that be all right?"

Without waiting for an answer, she helped him out of his coat and unfastened the many buttons on his vest. She let him take care of the gunbelt and made no effort to remove his shirt and trousers just yet. She guided him into the chair and knelt before him to tug his boots off.

"I'm not exactly used to this sort of attention," he said with a small smile as Wheezy knelt at his feet, her stiff leg jutting out to one side while her weight rested on her one good knee.

"Well, you should be. You are a beautiful man, Custis Long, and you deserve to be fussed over."

She set the boots aside and stripped off his socks. "Can you reach that bottle there? Pour yourself a drink, dear, while I massage your feet. You'll be surprised how refreshing that can be."

"Oh, I don't need—"

80

"No, dear, no one *needs* this kind of attention. But it will be good for you." Her smile was encouraging. "Trust me."

Longarm was not much of a brandy drinker, preferring his rye whiskey over pretty much anything else. But for brandy this stuff was not so bad. He had a swallow, the warmth of it bringing a sense of well-being to his body if not to his mind, while Wheezy sat on the floor and rubbed his feet.

And damned if the girl wasn't right. The gentle foot massage did make him feel remarkably refreshed and relaxed.

After a moment, the thoughts of that dead woman fell out of his mind and he began to pay attention to Wheezy again.

Some time during the past few minutes, without him ever particularly noticing it, she had shed the nightdress and now sat naked and pretty at his feet, her hair unpinned and falling in golden cascades onto her shoulders and down her back.

Longarm once again felt the stir of arousal.

Wheezy either saw or somehow sensed his readiness. Without comment, she abandoned the foot massage and ran her hands lightly up his calves and onto his thighs.

Her fingers deftly unfastened the buttons of his fly, and smiling, she spread the cloth wide.

Longarm's cock sprang to attention. He could feel Wheezy's breath warm on his flesh.

Then she dipped her head and he could feel much more than just her breath.

Her tongue was warm and gentle, her lips moist, encompassing.

Longarm groaned as the girl began, very gently at first and then with increasing urgency, to suck him.

He tried to remain motionless but that was a losing battle. He began lifting to meet her, driving himself ever deeper into her mouth, into her throat.

Wheezy began to make small whimpering sounds and to gobble wetly as she greedily demanded the fluids from his body.

And after a moment he could hold back no longer. Longarm felt the powerful surge deep in his groin, the gathering and then suddenly the explosion.

He poured his sap into Eloise Stephens's mouth, pumping a seemingly endless stream while she continued to suck, swallowing everything he had to give her.

He spilled himself completely into her. And then, drained, he slumped low in the hotel room chair.

"Lordy," he whispered.

Wheezy took his now-limp pecker in hand and pulled back to admire it lying there on her palm. A tiny, pearl-white drop of liquid oozed out, and with a smile she flicked her tongue to lift it away and swallow it along with the rest that had gone before.

Giggling happily, she looked up at him, her eyelashes long and lovely against the curve of her cheeks. She looked . . . happy. Genuinely happy.

"Tell me, sir. Are you relaxed now?"

"Somewhat," he admitted with a grin.

"Good, because you seemed ever so very tense when you came in."

"Reckon you took care of that," he said.

"Do you think you could take care of me now?" she boldly asked.

Longarm grinned at her. "Girl, I am gonna finish this here drink you gave me and maybe have a smoke. Then I am gonna carry you to that bed over yonder and see if I can make you pass out from the sheer pleasure of it all."

Her smile was impish. "Think you are man enough to do that?"

"Uh-huh."

Wheezy's smile became all the bigger. "Prove it!"

He did.

Chapter 20

They were at breakfast the following morning, Eloise eating little more than the smell off a piece of ham and Longarm doing the gentlemanly thing by helping her to finish it—along with his own meal of sausage, fried potatoes, flapjacks and eggs—when a bellboy came through the dining room.

"Mr. Long, please, Mr. Long."

"Here, boy."

The kid was probably barely into his teens, but he was old enough to appreciate beauty when he saw it. The note was for Longarm, but the boy's eyes were strictly for Wheezy. "Message for you, sir."

Longarm swapped him a nickel for the note and read it immediately, then passed it to Wheezy so she could see it, too. The *Willis Adams* was due to arrive in the early afternoon and would require repair before she could load passengers and freight for the haul up the Mississippi. She was scheduled to sail again the following morning at seven.

"We will have to stay here another night," Wheezy said. "I hope you don't mind."

Longarm looked at her and grinned. "Reckon I can stand more of this if you can."

Eloise's answering smile managed to give an impression of wide-eyed innocence. Which was quite a trick, considering. "The pleasure will be mine, sir."

She nibbled another tiny fleck of the salty ham, then said, "If you don't mind, I should like to have a little time to myself today. I've heard ever so much about the marvelous shops in St. Louis. They say you can find all the latest fashions, and I would like to see them even if I can't afford to buy them."

"Women like to do that sort of thing, don't you?"

"Well, yes. It really is not necessary to spend anything in order to enjoy shopping. Besides, I can feel of the material and see the way the cloth is cut and the seams laid out. Then perhaps one day I can make something similar for myself without spending much."

Eloise began to blush. And that was quite a trick, too, Longarm thought. An hour earlier this lovely girl had been naked and sweaty, driving him wild by licking his asshole. Now she sat here looking like a teenage virgin and blushing as red as a trainman's lantern.

"What?" he asked.

"I was wondering . . . while I am out . . . well, I need a few things. Female things, don't you see. It, well, it will soon be that time of month for me. And I . . . I need something."

"Yes?"

"But . . . Oh, bosh. This is so embarrassing."

"You're broke," he said, recalling why she'd asked to share the hotel room. "Is that it? D'you need a couple dollars?"

"Oh, not that much," she said quickly. "I don't want you to think . . ."

"Look, it isn't anything worth worryin' about. And Lord knows we been close enough lately that you oughta be able to ask me for a little help if you need it." He reached into his pocket and from the coins there selected a ten-dollar

84

eagle that he surreptitiously handed to her beneath the dining room table. "If you need more, just tell me."

Wheezy glanced at the coin in her palm and blushed all the harder. "I feel so cheap," she said. "I really should not take this."

He grinned. "Feel cheap, eh? Does that mean you want more'n that?"

"No, of course n—Custis! You are teasing me. You should not do that, dear. This is hard enough for me without you teasing me, too."

He laughed. "Sorry, little darlin'."

"You won't mind if I go off and shop today?"

"Of course not."

"You are welcome to come with me if you like," she said.

"Me? Go on a shoppin' binge with a woman? I don't think so, missy. But thank you for the invite."

"I may be gone all day," she said.

"That's all right. I can find something to do with myself. For one thing, getting that note reminds me that my boss probably thinks I'm in Wisconsin by now. I really oughta send a wire to bring him up to date. He might wanta notify the court down in Arkansas about the delay lest they expect to start the proceedings and not have their prisoner."

Wheezy made a face. "I know you explained it all to me, where you are going and why, but I simply do not understand all of those things."

"Sorry."

She smiled. "Really, dear, bonnets and gowns are ever so much more interesting than courts and prisoners and dreary things like that."

Longarm laughed. "Enjoy yourself today then with your bonnets and gowns and whatever."

"I shall, sir, and I trust you will enjoy your silly endeavors as well. If you would excuse me?"

"You haven't finished your breakfast."

"Could you be a dear and finish it for me, please?"

"Since you put it like that, I expect maybe I can." He stood and held Wheezy's chair while she gathered her bag and bonnet and limped away, managing somehow to move gracefully despite the handicap. Every male eye in the room followed her, then returned to give Longarm envious glances. She was quite the filly, little Eloise.

Longarm watched her out, then sat to resume his meal. And hers. Lordy, but she had damn near worn him completely out. He needed to stoke his boilers if they were going to have at it again tonight.

And he sure as hell hoped they were going to make the beast with two backs again come evening.

Chapter 21

"I need a couple things," Longarm told the clerk on duty at the Fairview's desk. "I want to send a telegram and I'd like to find a decent cigar store."

The clerk nodded. "Easily done, sir, for both of those. I can arrange to send your telegraph message, and I am told that Eller's is one of the finest cigar shops in the country. Would you like paper and pencil so you can compose your message? I can just add the cost of the telegram to your hotel bill and put it all on the government voucher."

Longarm nodded. "That'd be fine. And where is this Eller place?"

"Do you know the city, sir?"

"Not really."

"Then may I suggest you take a cab. Just tell the driver what you want. He is certain to know the place. It is quite famous."

"All right, thanks."

"I'll have the boy hail a hack for you as soon as you are done writing out your message then."

"You're mighty helpful."

"Happy to be of service, Marshal," the desk clerk said

with a smile. He handed over a lead pencil and a folio containing a thin sheaf of Western Union message forms.

Longarm carried the writing materials to a desk in the lobby and spent several minutes paring down his message to make it as brief as possible. Billy Vail hated having to pay for unnecessary verbiage in telegraph messages. After a minute or two Longarm grinned, crumpled up the form he'd been writing on and took out another.

"DELAYED STOP IN ST LOUIS END"

That said it all, he figured. The boss wouldn't be able to complain this time about never getting progress reports from Deputy Custis Long. Wouldn't be able, either, to respond with nit-picking orders and questions and shit since Longarm did not mention where he was or how long he expected to be there. And the message was sure as hell brief and to the point. No wasted words there, no sir. This was, Longarm calculated, just about the perfect progress report.

No, dammit, he'd gotten carried away with being overly wordy. The origin code would show where the wire came from. So there was no need to mention St. Louis, either. Longarm scratched that out and was left with only "DELAYED STOP."

Now it was perfect.

He just wished he could see Billy Vail's face when the marshal got this wire.

He carried his message form back to the desk and waited while the clerk sent the bellboy to summon a hansom to take him to this Eller's.

"I dunno," Longarm muttered more or less in the direction of the plump fellow behind the counter. "I'm thinkin' I may just have died an' gone on to heaven."

The entire wall behind that counter was a display. And the only objects on display were cigars. Wonderful cigars. Fabulous cigars. All manner of cigars, fat and slim, pale and dark. Lordy! What a store. No wonder it was famous.

Why, the scent alone was enough to put a man into ec-
stasy. The blending of smells from all those tobaccos was
finer than any perfume Longarm had ever encountered.
Better even than the smell of a good horse or new leather,
and those are scents a man can appreciate and enjoy.

"Are you Eller?"

"I am, sir." Eller was probably fifty-something with a
thick mop of gray hair and muttonchop whiskers that were
carefully brushed and full. He looked like a happy man.

"You know, Mr. Eller, comes the day I ever have to re-
tire and give up doing what I do, a place like this would be
mighty fine." He smiled. "But not here, of course. I
wouldn't want to go into competition with a gent who's
done so much to ease the lives of so many."

"That is laying it on a little thick, don't you think?"

"No, Mr. Eller, I mean it. A shop like this," Longarm extended his arm and pointed to all the glorious delights on
that wall, boxes open and slightly tilted so customers could
see what was on offer in each. "A shop like this, sir, is a
balm that improves the lot of the weary and gives joy to the
downtrodden. Wouldn't you agree?"

Eller laughed. "I have never had quite that reaction. But
I will say that I have customers who are some of the finest
gentlemen in Christendom. And if I do say so, I have some
of the finest cigars as well. I bring them up the river by way
of New Orleans, buy them from Cuba and Tampa and Do-
minica and several . . . those very dark, very full-bodied
flavor blunts . . . those come from Africa and these from
Mozambique."

Longarm shook his head in rapt appreciation. He meant
what he'd said, too. A shop like this could comfort a man if
he ever had to give up the active life.

"Can I direct you to something in particular?" Eller offered.

"I generally smoke these." Longarm pulled out one of the slim, dark little cheroots he'd bought at his favorite shop in Denver.

"May I?" Eller extended a hand and Longarm gave him the cheroot, which Eller peered at, then smelled of. "Nice, but . . ."

"I'm open to suggestion."

"Then may I recommend these. This is the Hernandez y Hernandez panatela. Very nice, I think." He pulled a box down off the wall, extracted one and handed it to Longarm. The cigar was rather long, sharply tapered at either end and made with a medium-brown outside wrapper leaf. "They are made by a gentleman, a Cuban actually, who does not get along well with the Spaniards who own and so badly oppress his island. He and a good many other dissident Cubans have settled in Florida. They've established a cigar industry there and are producing some very nice cigars. They buy their tobacco out of Cuba but blend and roll in Tampa. Very inexpensive, too, when you consider the quality. Would you like to try this one?"

The only response necessary was a huge smile from Longarm.

Eller very carefully clipped the twist with a gold cigar cutter, then placed the cigar onto a warmer that had a squat candle already burning beneath it. Eller let the tobacco warm, turning the cigar now and then to make sure the heat penetrated. When he was finally satisfied, he handed the smoke to Longarm and offered another candle—no match, of course, lest a hint of sulfur taint the purity of the tobacco—so Longarm could light it.

"Oh, my," Longarm groaned after he'd tasted the smoke. "That's better'n sex."

Eller grinned. "That depends on how much sex a man is getting, doesn't it?"

Longarm laughed. "Mr. Eller, I got to have some of

these." He did not even ask how much they cost. That did not matter. He intended to have them regardless.

"One box?"

"Two."

"May I suggest one box at a time then? It wouldn't do to allow these to dry out. I can always mail you more. Just drop me a note or a wire. I wax coat the boxes to seal in freshness and can send them anywhere."

"You can do that?"

"Oh, yes. I sell many, many more cigars than pass through that doorway. The gentlemen at the post office and I are on very good terms. Just give me your name and address and I shall create a file for you. Whenever you want a resupply, all you have to do is give me your name. I can look up your preference and fill the order."

"And payment?"

Eller shrugged. "I include a bill with the shipment. I've never had anyone cheat me afterward."

"Mr. Eller, sir, I have to tell you, it's a genuine pleasure being here and meeting you."

"Just write down the name and address then, and I will create an account for you."

Longarm was smiling when he picked up the offered pen and stiff file card that Eller laid on the counter before him.

Chapter 22

"Help you with that box, sir?"

Longarm paused, frowning for a moment, until he recognized the man who was standing on the sidewalk with his hand extended ready to take the cigar box from him. It was the same hack driver who had brought him to Eller's shop a little while earlier.

"I'm fine, thank you." It was only a box of cigars, after all, and certainly no great burden.

"Will you be going back to the hotel now, sir?"

"No, I don't think so. I got the day free. Think maybe I'll treat myself to a good meal to go with these fine cigars. D'you happen to know where a man can get a steak? Something top-notch now, grain-fed beef that's tender and juicy and full of flavor instead of your ordinary grass-fed beef."

"As a matter of fact I know the perfect place in the city if it's a steak you want. Well, close to the city if not exactly downtown. From here the drive might take close to an hour, but if you are not in a hurry . . ."

"I'm in no rush and the hour is still early anyhow."

"Then come with me, sir. My hack is just around the corner."

"You weren't waiting just for me, were you?"

"Actually, sir, I was not. I parked here waiting for another fare, but no else needed me before you came out. I saw you and kind of assumed you'd be wanting a ride again. I hope you don't mind."

"No, not at all." The driver held the door of his cab open, and Longarm climbed inside with his precious box of cigars. Damn, but they were fine.

"Very well, sir. If you need anything, sing out."

"Thank you."

The body of the light coach tilted sharply when the fellow climbed up onto the high driving box. There was a momentary pause, then Longarm heard him cluck to his team and they moved off with a slight lurch before settling into a smooth and easy trot.

Longarm sat back on the upholstery with one of those splendid—what had Eller called them? Hernandez y Hernandez or something like that; the name would be on the box when he unwrapped it—smoking one of his newfound cigars and enjoying the sights of the city as they drove away from the business district and headed south.

He smiled a little to himself. Free for the day, with nary a single obligation or duty to perform. A gorgeous and hot-blooded girl to enjoy at the end of the day. And these excellent panatela cigars. It just didn't get much better than that. No, sir, it did not.

Chapter 23

"I'll just cut across through these woods," the driver called down. "Save me more than a mile."

"That's fine," Longarm said.

The hack swung off the narrow road they'd been following and turned onto a bumpy track that wound through a thick stand of trees and emerged on top of a bluff overlooking the Mississippi. The view was spectacular. At least the natural part of it was. The human view was less than inspiring.

"Sorry about that, sir, but they paid me awful good."

"I see."

The problem was the trio of thugs who stood there waiting for the coach. Waiting, presumably, for one Custis Long, deputy United States marshal.

Longarm had never seen any of the three before. He was positive about that and had no idea what sort of beef they had with him. It must have been pretty extreme, though, because they were backing it up with revolvers and with the shotgun that one of them was holding.

The shotgun was an old model, a percussion muzzle loader with a single barrel that had been shortened so the gun could be easily concealed under a duster or even a coat. The shot pattern would spread to the point that it would be almost impossible to miss the target.

In this case the target of the man holding the shotgun seemed to be Longarm.

Longarm shuddered to think what might have been loaded into the barrel of that gun. Virtually anything small enough to fit into the muzzle could be used. And probably had been at one time or another. Carpet tacks were a particularly lethal and especially nasty load. They were too light to carry very far, but up close they would chop a man to shreds.

And this gun was close. The three were standing only five feet or so from the coach, two of them, including the one with the shotgun, beside the door and one on the opposite side.

"Out. Climb outa there, Long," one of them called.

Longarm scowled. They'd called him by name. This was not a chance encounter with robbers then. These men wanted him very much in particular, although he did not know why.

"Right now. Out."

The one standing at the window on the other side of the coach added, "Go ahead and draw your gun if you want to. If you think you're good enough to shoot both directions at once."

Longarm held his hands where they could be seen, and nodded at the door. One of the . . . what the hell were they if not robbers? Highwaymen? Assassins, more likely. One of them, the one on that side who had a pistol, obligingly opened the door for him while the one with the shotgun held it steady in the direction of Longarm's face.

He gave thought to carpet tacks and what a person looks like who has been shot with them. He could not help thinking about it.

He climbed meekly out of the coach, then stood with his hands raised.

The hack driver, that oh so helpful son of a bitch, whipped his team ahead. The coach rolled forward and swung around in the small clearing on top of the bluff, then bounced and rattled quickly away on the narrow path they'd taken to get there. It was out of sight in the dense woods within seconds.

The driver, Longarm surmised, did not want to be a witness to whatever was about to take place here.

Longarm figured he knew mighty well what was fixing to happen on this pretty site overlooking the broad, brown waters.

Or at least what these gents *thought* was fixing to happen.

Deputy Marshal Long had his own opinions as to how this ought to go.

The question now was . . . how the hell was he going to turn this thing around?

Chapter 24

"Just a second there, Kenny. Let us get his gun first."

It was the man with the shotgun who was doing the talking and who seemed to be in charge. That one was a rat-faced little piece of shit with stringy blond hair that came down over his collar. He stood about five foot three or four, and like so many short men looked like he carried a permanent chip on his shoulder, always ready to prove that he was as good a man as any. Except in this case he wasn't; the prick. Longarm glared at him.

The other one who had been standing close to the door when Longarm got out of the coach was taller and heavier built than Rat Face. He had a huge mustache and a beet-red complexion with prominent veins in his nose and cheeks that suggested he was an accomplished drunk. He looked dim-witted enough that he might not be really good at anything else, but, by jiminy, he could damn sure knock back the booze. The guy looked to be a champion in that area.

Kenny would presumably be the one who had been on the other side of the hack. Longarm had barely gotten a glimpse of him and then saw mostly the fellow's revolver, which was small and nickel plated, not much of a gun. Not much perhaps, but enough to kill a fellow.

Mustache circled out wide of Longarm and reached around from behind to snag Longarm's .44 out of its holster. Then he stepped back, remaining behind Longarm's back.

"Go on now, Kenny. You know what to do," Rat Face said, suggesting that Kenny probably was not as dumb as Mustache appeared to be.

Longarm heard the crunch of footsteps and a few moments later the sound of hoofbeats as a horse set off at a trot. That suggested there would be two other horses tied in the woods somewhere very close by.

Mustache remained behind Longarm while Rat Face was in front of him with the shotgun.

If Rat Face were to fire now, he very likely would cut down Mustache as well as Longarm. Somehow, though, that likelihood did not tempt Longarm into believing that Rat Face would hesitate to pull the trigger. He had the idea that Mustache was very probably an expendable chunk of muscle and not a valued member of this team. He damn sure was not inclined to stake his life on Rat Face's loyalty to his friends.

"This is a nice gun, Tommy," Mustache said.

"Keep it. It's yours."

"Gee, thanks. Thanks a lot." Mustache sounded pleased with the gift from Rat Face. Whose name obviously was Tom or Tommy.

Rat Face—Tommy—gestured with the shotgun. "Over there. By the cliff."

Longarm moved in the direction indicated and stood by the edge of a drop-off of thirty feet or more down to a narrow band of beach or bare riverbank at the edge of the Mississippi.

"Closer," Tommy said.

"I . . . Heights bother me. I might get dizzy and fall," Longarm said nervously.

"In that case, asshole, you'll die. Won't really bother me

all that much. Watch this guy, Quaker. I wanta get comfortable. We're prob'ly gonna be here for a while."

Quaker. It could have been his name, Longarm supposed. If it was a reference to his religion, though, the tenets of that faith hadn't taken root in this one.

Quaker frowned and concentrated on staring at Longarm while Tommy dropped into a cross-legged sitting position on the ground, his body angled a little so he could lay the shotgun across his lap while keeping it aimed in Longarm's direction.

"All right, Quaker. You can set down, too, if you want."

Quaker continued to stand, however.

"Mind if I ask a question?" Longarm said.

"You can ask. Maybe I'll answer. Maybe I won't."

"You can probably guess what I want to know. What's this all about?"

Tommy smirked and lightly stroked the barrel of his sawed-off. "We're waiting to see how much we can get for you. And whether it'll be more if you're dead or alive."

Longarm frowned. "Somebody wants me?"

"That's right."

"Who?"

"Now, I ain't gonna tell you a thing like that, mister. Not until all the bids are placed."

"Shit, you mean there's more than one?"

"Now, that's one of the things that we don't know, you see. But the word is out. Guy named Long. Your description. It's you, there's no doubt about it. Somebody has a price on you. Kenny's gone to get the rest of the information. Who and how many and for how much. If there's more than one, we'll hold us an auction. Of course if there's more than one and they both . . . or all of them in case there's a bunch . . . if they all want you dead, well, we can take care of that, too, and just collect from each of them. Wouldn't have to let the others know, if you see what I mean."

"Do I get a chance to get in on the bidding?" Longarm asked.

"You got money, mister?"

"Some. And I sure as hell have incentive to raise everything I can if that's what it takes to stay alive."

"Yeah, but you'd peach to the cops afterward if we was to just take your money and then turn you loose."

"I wouldn't have any proof against you, would I? It would be your word against mine. Three against one. I couldn't make anything stick even if I tried. And I'd give you my word not to try."

"I'll think about that," Tommy said. Then he smirked. "Maybe."

These jehus obviously did not know what Longarm did for a living, he realized. They seemed to think he was a businessman, possibly a gambler or a crook, someone who had aroused a certain amount of ire anyway. But he was fairly sure they had no idea they were dealing with the law here.

Quaker looked bored. His attention was wandering, and he kept peering off behind Longarm to the river and what was on it, or to the distant shore.

And Tommy's grip was relaxed on the small of the shotgun stock.

It was that shotgun that was worrisome. And it would only take a split second for Tommy to shift his grip and squeeze the trigger. At close range, it would be difficult for him to miss.

Longarm had had a vague notion about stepping backward off the edge to get away from the bastards. One quick look had been enough to convince him that was not the best of plans, however. The drop-off was too sheer for anyone to survive a fall without death or at the very least serious injuries, and the water was much too far away to reach should he try to dive from the bluff.

No, whatever he decided to do, it would have to be done here. With both Tommy and Quaker watching.

The good thing—if there could be said to be anything good about this situation—was that he seemed to have plenty of time. Kenny needed to go back to the city and make a number of inquiries before he came back to report to Tommy.

And the truth was that Longarm, too, would like to learn what Kenny found out in the city. Who the hell *was* after him? How many of them? And why?

On the other hand, if he saw an opportunity to extract himself from this predicament, it would be plain damn stupid for him to let the chance pass by untaken.

If he saw such a chance. If.

He stood there on the edge of the cliff, vulnerable to that damn shotgun, and . . . waited.

Chapter 25

"Don't get excited and do something foolish," Longarm said. "Like fire that scattergun. I'm gonna reach inside my coat for a cigar. You got my gun already. All I want now is a cigar. I'm, uh, just a little bit nervous here."

"You don't need no cigar."

"Look, you don't know what the deal is here and maybe you'd be passing up a lot of money by shooting when you don't need to. And all I want is a damn cigar. I promise not to hit you with it."

"Quaker. You give him the cigar. I don't want his hands going nowhere that I can't see them."

"Me? Jeez, Tommy, I don't have no seegars."

"Give him one of his own cigars, you dumb fuck."

"Tommy, I don't have . . ."

"You get off your fat ass and walk over there, Quaker. The man takes his coat off an' hands it to you. Then you get one of his cigars an' give it to him. While you're at it, you can bring me a cigar, too. Hell, have one for yourself if you want."

"You know I don't smoke, Tommy."

"Then chew the thing. Or don't take one, I don't give a shit. Now go get the man's coat."

Tommy motioned with the barrel of the shotgun. "You. Off with the coat. But real careful. You hear me? Real damn careful or I'll cut you in half and prob'ly your cigars along with the rest of you."

"Real careful," Longarm agreed. He held his arms wide, then very gingerly used two fingers on his left hand to grip the lapel and pull his tweed coat off that shoulder. He put his left arm down and allowed the coat to fall of its own weight.

"That's fine," Tommy said. "Now the other side."

Longarm shrugged his right shoulder and let his coat fall to the ground, leaving him standing in his vest and shirtsleeves.

"Quaker, get the coat and gimme a cigar."

"You want me to give him one, too?"

"Yeah, I want you to give him one, too."

Quaker walked in front of Longarm, apparently forgetting about the threat of that shotgun, and retrieved Longarm's coat from the ground. Longarm was not even tempted to use that momentary screening, though, as an opportunity to make his break. Tommy saw where Quaker was headed and was all too intent on watching Longarm.

"There's four seegars here," Quaker said.

"Give the man one an' bring me one."

"Whadda you want me to do with the others?"

"Leave them there."

"What about the coat?"

"Just drop it. Shit, Quake, do I hafta tell you everything?"

Quaker extracted one of Longarm's fine panatelas and handed it to him, then dropped the coat as instructed and carried another cigar to Tommy.

"Don't stand between me an' him," Tommy instructed.

"Oh. Yeah." Quaker grinned and moved well to the side so he would not be in the line of fire if Tommy let go with that shotgun.

"There. That wasn't so hard now, was it?" Tommy mumbled.

Longarm bit the twist off the end of his panatela and took a moment to inhale the aroma of the tobacco leaf, then moistened the newly exposed tip by rolling the cigar around in his mouth before finally planting it between his teeth.

"Careful," Tommy warned, again gesturing with the muzzle of the shotgun for entirely unnecessary emphasis.

Longarm nodded, his concentration apparently on nothing more threatening than that cigar.

He dipped two fingers into his vest pocket.

Chapter 26

Tommy never even saw the little brass-framed .41 derringer Longarm dug out of his vest pocket. The diminutive
pistol had twin barrels and was soldered to the end of Longarm's watch chain. It made for a dandy watch fob. It was
also useful for other things. Like now.

Proper procedure here would be for Deputy Marshal
Long to identify himself and in a commanding voice in-
struct Tommy and Quaker to surrender because they were
now under arrest.

Right. You bet. And in that case, Tommy would yank the
shotgun trigger and ruin Longarm's whole day.

Procedure be damned. Longarm thumbed back the
hammer of the little gun and raised it in one swift motion,
sighting down the top barrel of the derringer toward the
bridge of Tommy's nose.

Quaker, damn him, saw what was happening before
Tommy ever did. And while Quaker might indeed be a big,
dumb, muscle-bound oaf, he proved to be a very quick oaf.
He spotted the derringer and sprang toward Longarm.

Longarm squeezed gently on the derringer's spur trigger, and the little gun barked, its sound magnified out of all
proportion by the shortness of the barrels.

The .41-caliber lead slug entered Tommy's left eye and very messily rearranged the shape of the man's head.

Tommy was no longer alive to know it, but he did manage to fire the shotgun, his finger jerking involuntarily in a death spasm. The shotgun roared and a spray of pellets— or carpet tacks, dimes, something—swept the ground to Longarm's right.

Longarm's thumb went to the hammer of the derringer for that second shot, but he did not have time to cock the pistol. Quaker was already too close and charging.

Longarm darted to his left, very much mindful of the cliff that was not more than two paces behind him, but Quaker did not oblige him by rushing past and off the cliff. The big man adjusted his direction with all the agility of a cat and launched himself at Longarm.

The two of them went to the ground hard, Quaker's considerable weight on top and driving the air from Longarm's lungs.

Quaker began digging short, vicious punches into Longarm's ribs, grunting with the effort as he did so. His breath huffed and whistled in Longarm's right ear.

Quaker needed to clean his teeth. And he really should not eat that much damn garlic.

The man gave the impression that he was settling into a rhythm that he could maintain for a very long time if need be. And those body blows hurt like hell.

Worse, if they kept up, Longarm knew it was only a matter of time before ribs started to break.

Longarm pulled his hand out from under Quaker, but instead of trying to block some of those punishing body blows, he cocked the derringer, shoved it into Quaker's gut and pulled the trigger.

The sound of the gunshot was muffled by Quaker's body. He stiffened and cried out, the rain of punches ceasing.

"You've killed me, you son of a bitch." He reached for Longarm's throat with both hands.

Quaker was a powerful man, but his strength was quickly waning. Longarm dropped the derringer and pushed Quaker away, rolling the big man off of him.

Shaken and hurting badly from the punishment Quaker had gotten in before Longarm was able to shoot him, Longarm took a moment to stand with his hands braced on his knees, sucking air into his lungs and trying to recover his strength. Lordy but that Quaker could hit.

Longarm retrieved the derringer and tucked it back into his vest pocket. He did not have any spare cartridges for that gun with him. Those were in his bag back at the hotel.

He had no idea what had become of the cigar he'd been about to light when this whole thing got started. He looked around for a moment but did not see the panatela. He still had a few in his coat, though, and . . .

Aw, *shit*! His precious box of Hernandez y Hernandez was still in the backseat of that damn hansom cab.

Which served as one more reason to look up the cab-driver and have a word or two with the son of a bitch.

Longarm straightened up and stretched, then drew in a long, satisfying breath.

He figured he could brush himself off a little and re-trieve his coat and Colt and go help himself to one of the horses he expected to find in the woods nearby.

Then . . .

It was the sound of gravel crunching underfoot that saved him.

Quaker, incredibly, had found the strength somehow to wobble upright and make one last lunge at his final enemy.

He came at Longarm like a wounded animal, dying but still lethal, knowing he was as good as dead but determined to take Longarm with him . . . determined to take Longarm with him over the edge of the cliff, damn him.

Quaker held his arms wide as if to scoop Longarm up, and charged silently forward.

Longarm threw himself to the side, hitting the ground with his shoulder and rolling out of the way.

Quaker had already used up all his reservoirs of strength just to get to his feet and make that desperate lunge. He could not stop himself. Or possibly did not bother to try. Whatever the reason, he swept past Longarm and grimly, silently over the edge of the cliff.

There was a pause that seemed to take forever and then, finally, the ugly thump of a heavy body striking the earth all that distance below.

Longarm shook his head and felt of his ribs, hoping none of them was busted, before he moved rather shakily to the edge of the cliff and looked down.

Quaker, damn him, looked scarcely human from this perspective. The body could as easily have been a bundle of rags as a once human creature.

And the bastard still had Longarm's .44 on him. Longarm was going to have to find a way down there to retrieve it before he could start back to the city.

For a day that had started out so very nicely, things had turned to shit in a big hurry.

He could get along with that, though. Standing here being annoyed was a helluva lot better than lying in Tommy's place or Quaker's. Yes, sir, Longarm figured he would take this over dying just any old time.

He picked up his coat and slipped it on, spotted the panatela on the ground and retrieved it, too. He reached into his vest pocket, this time bringing out a match, and lighted the cigar.

Damn but that was good.

It was good, too, to be alive. Very, very good.

Chapter 27

"You could at least have brought the bodies in with you," the overweight and aging desk sergeant grumbled.

"Like hell," Longarm told him. "There was no way I was gonna drag that big sonuvabitch to the top of that bluff. It was tough enough getting myself down there and back up again. I figure you can send a boat down to collect him. The other one, too. Just look for a dead guy lying along the riverbank. The one called Quaker will be the only one there." Longarm paused for a moment to consider. "Well, probably."

The police sergeant looked quite put-upon, but he said, "All right. I will tend to it. Is there anything else?"

"No other bodies if that's what you mean."

"It is. Your count is up to three now. That seems to be quite enough."

"Look, I'm perfectly willing to leave all the local criminals to you. Just tell them to quit trying to stab me or shoot me or whatthefuckever. I do have a question for you, though. It's about these horses. D'you want to impound them or something?"

"I recognize the ear brand. They belong to a livery over

on the west side. I'll see they get back where they belong. The saddles go with them, or do you want those?"

"The saddles go with the horses I'd reckon. I sure don't have any use for them. You, uh, wouldn't have any idea who the missing one is, would you?"

"Kenny, you said his name is?"

"That's what Tommy called him. He had a horse, too. Likely rented from the same stable as these two."

"I'll have my boys look into that. Could be the folks at the livery will be able to help. If I find him, what should I do?"

"Arrest the bastard. The charge will be attempted murder of a federal peace officer. I'll be at the Fairview until tomorrow morning. After that, you can send me a wire in care of my boss in Denver. And yes, I damn sure will file charges against him. If you do get him, though, try and find out what he knows about that price on my head. I wouldn't mind trading his freedom for that little piece of information."

"Can I tell him that?"

"Hell, yes. But he doesn't walk until I have a chance to verify what he says. I don't want him making somethin' up and then going on the trot."

"Teach your grandmother to suck eggs, Deputy. I've been in this business since you were in diapers. Maybe longer."

"Sorry. I meant no offense."

"None taken," the local cop said. "And don't worry. If I come up with anything, I'll send a runner to the hotel for you."

"Thanks."

Longarm excused himself and found another cab. He thought about trying to locate the same fellow who had driven him this morning, if for no other reason to recover his Tampa panatelas. It seemed unlikely that he would be able to locate that slimy gentleman among all the many cabs in the city, so he settled for making another trip to Eller's.

"Goodness. Back so soon," Eller greeted him.

"I need another box of the Hernandez y Hernandez. I, uh, managed to misplace them others."

"Your tone of voice suggests there is a story you don't feel like telling."

"You could say that," Longarm agreed.

"No matter. Let me get another box for you."

Longarm paid for his purchase—although if he kept on losing them, this cigar habit could become decidedly expensive—and left the store. Again.

This time he walked several blocks before hailing a cab and telling the driver to take him to the Fairview. Not that he expected a repeat of the attempted kidnap earlier. But it never hurts to be careful.

He was back at the hotel in time for a late lunch. There was no sign of Wheezy in their room, so Longarm went out again and off in search of a quiet saloon—*not* the same one from last night where the knife-wielding whore found him, thank you—and the quieter the better. Longarm had had about a belly full of St. Louis's criminal element.

But he certainly did wonder who wanted him dead. And why.

Chapter 28

Longarm was contented. And about as thoroughly satiated as it was possible for one human person to get. He felt positively hollow, from his navel to his knees. Wheezy Stephens had dragged him up to their room immediately after supper and acted like she was bent on draining every last drop of fluid out of him.

And, he thought with a grin, she'd pretty much done it. He couldn't recall ever before making it so often or so powerfully. Time after time and one position after another. Wheezy was insatiable. Which Custis Long did not mind the least little bit.

Now Longarm lay in the dark in the middle of the night, physically exhausted but wide awake. Wheezy lay snuggled warm at his side, her naked body pressed lightly against his. He could feel her breathing quite as easily as he could hear it.

He smiled. At least now Eloise's renown after-sex, after-exertion wheezing had subsided and her breathing was back to normal. She was quite the girl, little Wheezy. Good to look at and a wildcat in bed. She was a regular sex machine, and if he could get a patent on her, he could make a fortune turning out similar models for the gentry.

117

But then there could not be another one like Wheezy. That simply wouldn't be possible, not in a thousand years. Wheezy was one of a kind.

Longarm closed his eyes, determined to get some sleep, but for some reason he was unable to drop off.

Nothing was bothering him. Was it?

Oh, he was concerned about this thing about there being a price on his head in the St. Louis underworld. Not so much the fact of it—he lived with that sort of defiance and fear from the criminal element every day of his life—as the idea that he had no notion of why.

That was not the sort of thing that would keep him awake, though. He'd long ago learned to deal with what was before him and not fret himself with the possibilities of things that had not happened.

No, it was something else that was keeping him awake now. He was sure of it.

He lay in the dark, eyes wide open and hands laced behind his neck, listening to Wheezy's soft breathing and to the few distant street sounds coming in through the open window. A flimsy curtain billowed uncertainly at a puff of cool night air.

Wheezy's skin was pure silk, Longarm mused. Cool to the touch. Most places. Burning hot and slippery wet in others.

And that mouth of hers. . . . Longarm felt a stirring of arousal, something he would not have thought possible after the workout he'd given the blind snake earlier in the evening.

Yes, sir, helluva girl that Wheezy.

He pondered the idea of waking her up and making the beast with two backs one more time.

She was tired, though. Hell, so was he. Exhausted was more like it. But not completely limp. He smiled a little into the dark at that thought.

Probably he'd be better off finding his coat—where the

hell had she dropped it, anyway; across the room, wasn't it—and having a panatela. That should settle him down and let him sleep. And while he was over there on the other side of the hotel room, he could retrieve his gunbelt. Wheezy had done most of the undressing for both of them, and she had stashed his Colt and gunbelt on the floor between the chair and the wardrobe. He'd made a mental note of that at the time.

And now that he was thinking about it, that was the little thing that was nagging at him and keeping him from getting to sleep.

His .44 was way the hell out of reach should he need it in the night. And there was a price on him in this town. Now, wasn't that a disquieting thought. No damn wonder he wasn't sleeping.

The thing he'd have to do, he figured, was to slip out of bed—hopefully without waking Wheezy—and drape his gunbelt over the bedpost where it belonged. A gun that is out of reach or unloaded is of no damn use to anyone, and if one is needed, it is needed damned well right *now,* not later on.

That was exactly what he needed to do, he decided.

He very gently lifted the sheet and laid it on top of the slender girl's sleeping form. He was about to slip out of the bed when he heard a faint scraping sound at the open window and saw a shadow pass across that opening.

Something moving just outside? They were on the third floor, for Pete's sake, and there was no balcony.

Yet . . .

A dark shape filled the lower part of the window, and a hand reached inside to push the curtain aside.

Longarm heard a soft, metallic clink—a hook or buckle being disengaged perhaps?—and the intruder silently slithered into the room.

Longarm felt a chill. What was it he'd just been thinking? That a gun out of reach is of no use at all?

119

Well, that was for damn sure true.

He was lying naked in bed, and someone, a thief or more likely an assassin, was standing between him and his Colt .44.

Shee-damned-it!

Chapter 29

There seemed no point in lying there waiting to be shot or stabbed or bludgeoned, and at least for the moment the intruder would be thinking Longarm was asleep and unaware of his presence.

Surprise being the only real weapon he had available, Longarm used it. He took a slow, deep breath and then sprang from the bed with an ear-shattering roar.

The intruder recoiled in shock, and Longarm was on him, striking out for his hands. He heard a distinctively metallic clatter on the floor. The sound suggested the man was armed with a heavy knife or perhaps a short pry bar. The pry bar was a likely choice actually, as it could be used to jimmy a closed window or to shatter the skull of a sleeping victim. Whatever the intruder had been carrying was on the floor now, lost in the darkness.

Longarm's weight bore the man down, and both of them fell to the floor kicking and punching.

The bastard tried to knee Longarm in the balls. He felt it coming and managed to take it on his thigh instead.

While the intruder was doing that, Longarm was driving short, hard punches into the man's ribs and belly, putting all his weight and muscle behind the blows and grunting with effort. He thought he heard the muted crunch of a rib breaking, and the intruder cried out in pain, then tried the knee again with no better result than the first time.

The fellow was hurting but he was game. Longarm had to give him that much. He kept squirming and thrashing, trying to hit, trying to bite. Longarm abandoned his assault on the man's ribs and responded to the biting with the heel of his hand jammed in an uppercut to the underside of the fellow's jaw. That, too, brought a cry of pain. Longarm suspected there may have been a bit of tongue trapped between the guy's teeth when they bashed together. If so, he would be talking funny for a week or so.

The intruder had clearly gone on the defensive at this point and was struggling, not so much to overcome Longarm as to get the hell away from him.

Longarm was not about to let that happen. He wanted this guy. Wanted to question him about who sent him here and why.

Longarm managed to get an arm around him and flipped him over so the intruder was facedown on the floor. Longarm grabbed hold of one flailing wrist and yanked it behind the guy's back hard enough that it was a wonder he didn't break it. Not that he really would have cared if he did. That would only have made the son of a bitch that much easier to handle. Grab hold of an already broken arm and you can convince someone to hold still without a whole hell of a lot of additional effort.

"Leave be, you piece of shit," Longarm snarled. "Quit wiggling and give me the other arm."

The fellow kicked and twisted, but Longarm had his arm levered painfully high behind his back and every movement had to cost the man a terrible price of pain.

All the screaming and banging had not gone unnoticed elsewhere in the hotel. Loud voices in the hallway demanded entrance, and a few seconds later someone or something crashed into the door and broke the lock open.

Light from the hallway flooded into the room and half a dozen men with it. Longarm and his captive were illuminated. The intruder turned out to be a slender, wiry fellow with sleek black hair, a pencil mustache and an olive complexion. He was wearing dark, close-fitting clothing that would be just the thing for escaping notice in the night. Longarm was positive he had never seen the man before.

"What the hell is this about?" someone loudly demanded.

"Damn if I know," Longarm started to say, "but this fella—"

His words were cut short by a very loud bang and a brief flash of light.

The intruder's head snapped back and he went limp. For a moment Longarm could not see why the hell the man was down, although Wheezy was sitting upright in bed holding a dinky little Colt .22 revolver.

And the intruder had been drilled quite neatly in one eye. The tiny bullet had obviously gotten inside the man's skull, and likely rattled around in there until it ran out of steam. No wonder the son of a bitch was dead. Longarm turned loose of the fellow's wrist—he was no threat to anyone now—and stood up.

"What the hell'd you do that for?"

"He was reaching for that . . . club thing or whatever it is," Wheezy said. She sounded quite calm. And seemed completely unaware that she was sitting there every bit as naked as Longarm, in full view of the men who had come rushing into the room. Those lucky sons of bitches were getting an eyeful, leering now at probably the prettiest girl they would ever in their lives get a chance to see in the nude.

Longarm had seen her already and turned his attention to the dead man on the floor. His outstretched arm, the one he had not surrendered to Longarm, lay almost on top of the short steel pry bar he'd brought into the room with him.

Longarm could see now that the intruder also had a

knife sheathed at his waist, where he could have gotten to it all too easily.

Longarm still thought he'd had the fellow under control. But Wheezy would not have known that.

"Fellows, thanks for coming to help, but I'm a U.S. deputy marshal and things are in hand. You can leave now." He reached to take his wallet and badge out before he remembered that he, too, was jaybird naked.

"Everybody out now. Thanks, though. Thanks for helping. Go along." He positioned himself so that he was between all those eagerly staring eyes and Eloise Stephens's perky tits, and shooed the spectators back into the hallway.

Longarm dragged the chair over to prop against the door. The latch had been busted when the neighbors broke in.

He lighted first the lamp and then a cigar. Then he sat down on the side of the bed and sighed.

"Did I do good, Custis? Is everything all right now?"

"Yeah, baby." He reached for Wheezy and pulled her to him. "You did good." He smiled and lied, "You saved my life there, y'know." She hadn't, of course. The guy had been lying facedown on the floor and Longarm had had him in an armlock. He would not have been going anywhere or swinging any pry bar.

But to be fair, the fellow might have been able to get to that knife. So maybe she had saved him after all. Sort of.

Whether she had or not really did not matter, though. She'd tried. Hell, she'd killed a man to protect Longarm. He had to appreciate that.

He held her close and kissed her long and deeply.

Getting the dead guy out of the room could wait just a little while longer, he decided.

Chapter 30

The St. Louis constable who showed up to investigate the shooting was the same one who had been on the scene when the whore named Sarah tried to knife Longarm.

"I have to say, sir, that you have an unfortunate ability to draw trouble to yourself."

"That's one way to put it, but there's no question what happened here. The guy broke in. I jumped him. You can see the rest for yourself." He did not think it would be right to mention that it was Wheezy who actually shot the SOB. That would only complicate matters to no purpose.

"Yes, sir. Oh, by the way. Are you still interested in that man you were looking for the other night? The gambler who had a grudge?"

"Yes, of course."

"I asked around, sir. I found out who he is."

"Good for you. You said your name is George?"

"Yes, sir."

"You did well, George. You wouldn't happen to know where this fella lives, would you?"

"Yes, sir, that's one of the things I learned. He stays at a rooming house about three blocks from here."

"Let's go pay the gentleman a call."

"Now, sir? It is . . ." He fumbled a watch out of his pocket and looked at it. "It is half past three in the morning."

"Yes, and pretty soon it will be four. And pretty soon after that I have to show up at the quay and catch a steamer. I'd like a chance to question this fella before I go."

"But what about . . . you know." He motioned to the body on the floor.

"Hell, we'll drag it out in the hall and tell the desk clerk to call someone to carry it off. George, old son, you worry too much about the dead ones. It's the living that can cause you trouble." Longarm pulled on his coat and turned to Wheezy.

"Will you be all right here by yourself or should I have the hotel send a bellboy or somebody up to keep you company?"

"I'm fine, dear. You go on and do whatever you have to do. I . . . I hope you get whoever was behind these awful attacks on you. Get him and shoot him down."

Longarm gave Eloise a goodbye kiss—after all, they were supposed to be husband and wife, at least so far as the hotel was concerned—and followed the young policeman downstairs.

"The door is locked," the cop said. "Should I break in?"

"No. We don't have cause for that. I'm gonna go around back to nab anybody that tries to sneak out. Give me a minute or two, then knock on the door to wake somebody and get in. Remember, though. Once you do get in, let me in by the back way. I'll want to have my words with this fella."

George nodded his understanding, and Longarm went around to the back of the narrow two-story boardinghouse. There were no lamps burning inside. The place was dark and silent.

Longarm mounted the steps to the back porch and tried that door. Often folks would lock their front door to keep

126

out thieves but leave the back open so the residents could get out to the shitter rather than use the awkward and smelly thunder mugs for nocturnal relief.

No such luck this time. The back door was as securely locked as the front. Longarm helped himself to a seat on a stool he found on the porch and waited. A minute or so later he heard George banging loudly at the front and calling out for entry.

The racket continued for a good five or six minutes—a hellacious long time in the middle of the night—before finally someone responded. Even from as far away as the back porch Longarm could overhear George announce himself.

"This is the police. I'm here to question one of your boarders."

That, Longarm figured, should spook any rats in this nest.

Sure enough, within seconds he heard a thump overhead as someone slipped out a second-floor window onto the porch roof. Longarm smiled and waited for him. The fellow lowered himself over the edge of the roof and waved his legs around until he found the thin support pillar, then transferred his weight to that and lowered himself hand over hand to the porch.

Where Longarm waited.

"Goin' somewhere?" Longarm said mildly.

"Aaghh!" The man jumped clean out of his skin. Longarm took hold of his wrist, spun him around and clamped handcuffs onto him.

He was thin and dark, not very large, and was barefoot. He was wearing an undershirt and trousers. He had taken time to fasten his belt so his britches would not fall off, but he had not buttoned his trousers.

Longarm had never seen him before.

"Who the hell are you?" he asked.

"I, uh . . . I . . ."

"Never mind." The guy would only lie to him anyway, Longarm figured, and he did not much care to be lied to. A good, honest silence was much better to his mind than the cleverest lie. And this fellow sure as hell did not seem a very clever sort.

Still, he had some reason to run from the police. Longarm led him over to the back door, where soon he could see the bobbing approach of a shielded lamp, the person carrying it still in darkness so that it looked like the light was floating down a hallway and across the kitchen to the back door.

"Are you Long?" the man with the lamp asked. "The policeman said I should let you in. Peter, what are you doing here?"

"You know this fellow?" Longarm asked.

"Of course. He is one of my boarders. Peter Branvold. He isn't in any trouble, is he? Is Peter the reason you officers are here?"

"He isn't the reason I'm here. I dunno about George." Longarm turned to his prisoner. "What're you running from anyway?"

Branvold remaining sullenly silent, head down as if intent on studying his toenails. Which badly needed trimming.

"Come along." Longarm took Branvold to the front of the rooming house. "Is this fella anything to you, George?"

The St. Louis cop studied the fellow's face for a moment, then shook his head.

"His name is Branvold. Peter."

"Never heard of him," George said.

Longarm turned him around and removed the handcuffs. "Go back to bed, mister." To George he said, "Now, where's the guy we came here to see?"

"Top floor on the left," George said, leading the way.

Longarm drew his Colt and held it ready before he followed.

Chapter 31

"Oh, my god. Please. Please don't shoot me, I ... What are *you* doing here?" The poker player was wearing a pair of socks and nothing else. A lamp, its wick turned low and flame shielded to allow only a little light, was pulled very close to the bed.

And beside it there was an open box containing a thick sheaf of pasteboard cards. A stereopticon lay on the bed, one of the cards fitting into it.

Longarm picked up the stereopticon while George handcuffed the prisoner. Longarm turned up the lamp wick to allow more light and looked into the viewing device. Then he laughed.

"D'you know what we interrupted, what our guy was doing when we came in? He was looking at dirty pictures and beating his meat."

"What?"

"Shit, it's true. Wait until you see this picture. Two naked women and a guy with a hood over his head. What's in ... Dear me, George. The rest of these cards are just as dandy. Here's one with a donkey and a ... Shit, I never knew a woman could handle something like that." He shook his head. "Just goes to prove the old saying, George. You're never too old to learn something new."

"Let me see those."

"Look, I . . . I . . . Those are private," the man in the handcuffs stammered.

"Which they damn sure ought to be," Longarm agreed.

"These are illegal," George said. "Bound to be."

Longarm scowled. "Personally I don't give a rat's ass about a bunch of French postcards, and if this guy wants to spend his nights fucking Mamie Five Fingers, that's perfectly all right by me. But when he starts hiring killers, that's another story." He turned to the prisoner. "Your name is Benson? Roger Benson?"

Benson looked awfully uncomfortable standing there wearing nothing but the handcuffs and black socks. "Yes, but . . . who are you?"

"You know damn good and well who I am."

"No, I . . . I mean, I recognize you, of course. We played cards the other night. You cheated me then."

"Mister, you lost. That don't mean I cheated."

"But what are you . . . ? Why did you bring a policeman to break in here? I haven't done anything to you."

"You know who I am and what you've done," Longarm accused.

Benson turned to George. "Officer! Please. Why are you arresting me? What have I done?"

"You hired those killers, didn't you?"

Benson looked genuinely puzzled. "Killers? I don't know what you are talking about."

"The other night," Longarm said. "You hired a whore named Sarah to put a knife in my back."

"Sarah? You're the one who killed Sarah?"

"After she tried to knife me, yes, I damn sure did."

"I heard she was dead."

"You admit that you knew her?"

"Mister, everybody around this end of town knows . . .

130

knew . . . Sarah. I used her myself sometimes. Probably would have had her or one of them like her the other night if I hadn't lost all my money to you. Now I'm behind in my rent and can't even afford a shave."

Longarm frowned and stepped into the hall, where the anxious boardinghouse proprietor was nervously waiting, probably worrying about what all of this would do to his reputation and that of his place.

"Is that right, mister? Is Benson here too broke to pay his rent this week?"

"That's right. I charge four dollars and a half each week or sixteen by the month. He paid me two dollars this week. Said something about losing the rest at poker." The guy shrugged. "This has happened a couple times before. I know he's good for it. He'll stay out of the saloons until he catches up on his rent, then he'll go back to his wicked ways."

"Benson doesn't have a lot of money to throw around then?" Longarm was thinking about that shiny double eagle they found in Sarah's pocket.

"Good Lord, no."

Longarm was scowling when he went back inside Roger Benson's room. "Damn!"

"What's wrong, Marshal?" George asked.

"Marshal? This guy is some kind of marshal? Oh, God." Benson looked like he was going to pass out.

"You really don't know who I am?" Longarm asked.

"As God is my witness, no," Benson declared.

"Unfortunately I believe you," Longarm said. To the St. Louis policeman he added, "I hate to say this, George, but we've broke in on the wrong guy. Benson isn't the one behind all this trouble."

"What about those pictures?" George asked, nodding toward the stereopticon and the box of lewd photographs.

"They aren't against any federal law that I know about. You can do anything you like, but if it was me I'd let this

131

poor son of a bitch go back to beating his meat and imagining he was one of the guys in those pictures."

George turned Benson around and unlocked the manacles. "Put a nightshirt on or something, will you. It's almost my dinnertime and you're taking my appetite away."

Benson scuttled to the bedside and hid his collection of smut and the three-dimensional viewer for it under the sheet, never mind that it was much too late for that. He reached for a pair of trousers draped over a chair nearby, but by then Longarm and the policeman were already on their way out.

"I'm sorry this didn't work out," George said.

"So am I, but you certainly did your job," Longarm told him. "I have to leave this morning, don't want to miss my boat upriver, but I'd like for you to give me the name of your commander. I'll send him a note to tell him how much help you've been and what a good job you did."

George beamed. "Do you mean that?"

"Of course I do. You deserve the compliment, and it'll do you more good going to your chief than just me telling you."

"Gosh, maybe I could even get a day shift and have hours like a regular human being. Working nights all the time makes me feel like a bat or something."

"Give me the man's name," Longarm said, "and I'll write that note quick as I get back to the Fairview."

"Yes, sir. Thank you."

Custis Long, however, was considerably less pleased as they traveled the dark streets back toward the hotel. He still did not know who was behind those attacks on him. Or why. Dammit.

Chapter 32

"I'm glad enough to be seein' the last of St. Louis," Longarm admitted as he and Wheezy stood at the rail of the *Willis Adams* watching the city fall behind them. The long, rather racy boat splashed noisily forward, churning against the current, the power of the engine relentless.

"So will I." She shuddered. "This morning . . . that man . . . It was awful. Just awful."

Longarm hesitated, thinking she might not welcome a public display of affection now that they were aboard the paddlewheeler and back in separate cabins, but Wheezy pressed herself tight to his side as if in need of comfort, so he accommodated by wrapping his arms around her. The pretty girl sighed and rested her cheek against his chest.

"Custis, dear."

"Yes?"

"I hope . . . Can I sneak over and visit you sometimes? I will be discreet. Really." Hastily she added, "I will try not to be a burden to you. And if you have other . . . company . . . for the evening, if you see what I mean . . . I'll not say a word. I promise. I mean, I am not making any claims on your time. But I would like . . . if you would be willing . . ."

He smiled and lightly kissed the top of her head. "I can't imagine your presence bein' a burden to anybody, and I'll always be happy to see you." He smiled and glanced around to make sure there were no other passengers close enough to overhear before he added, "With or without clothes on."

"Thank you, dear, thank you," she murmured into the rough tweed of his coat. She put both arms around him, right there on the promenade deck, and hugged him. There were several gentlemen on deck and a handful of women. Longarm figured for the rest of this voyage he would be the object of considerable envy from the men and at least an equal amount of condemnation from the ladies. But that was all right. Come nightfall he was the one would be enjoying the many delights this girl had to offer. And Lord knew those pleasures were many and deep.

"Hungry?" he asked. By the time Wheezy was packed and ready to go this morning, they had had to hurry to get to the quay and had no time for breakfast at the Fairview.

She smiled. "For you."

"I meant for food."

Wheezy giggled. "I would rather eat you."

"Now, get serious."

"Your juice tastes ever so much better than coffee. Did you know that, dear?"

"I meant . . ."

"This afternoon. Can I drink your juice this afternoon, dear?" She lifted her face to him, looking innocent and virginal. She fluttered her eyelashes outrageously and then winked at him. "Can I, please?"

"What the hell am I gonna do with you," he groaned.

"Oh, I can think of a few things," Wheezy said.

"Don't I know it."

"You never said if I can have you this afternoon. In my mouth. I want the taste of you in my mouth and the feel of you deep in my throat. Will you do that for me? Please?"

"Keep your voice down. Somebody's gonna hear."

"Will you? You have to promise. Will you do that?"

Longarm looked around. The two of them definitely had the attention of the other passengers on the open deck. If those folks could hear . . .

"Promise me, Custis. Promise." She pursed her lips into a pout.

"I, uh, all right, I promise."

Wheezy laughed happily at that and clapped her hands. Anyone watching might have thought he'd just given her a present.

"Now can we go down to the dining salon?"

"Oh, I hope so," Wheezy said. "I am starving. Simply *starving*."

Women, Longarm thought. How the hell d'you figure them?

Chapter 33

Longarm's legs were weak. Genuinely, seriously, honest-to-Pete wobbly in the knees. That was not just an expression. With Wheezy Stephens, a man was so thoroughly used up that there was just not a whole hell of a lot left over for other purposes. By the time Longarm made it out of her cabin that afternoon, it was close to suppertime. And he was close to exhaustion.

"Now, don't you be worrying about me," she'd told him, all bright and fresh and filled with energy. She came onto tiptoes to give him a kiss and a pat on the butt. "I won't be going in to supper, I think. I will ring the steward and tell him I have the vapors or something. I know he will bring a light supper to my cabin. And hot water. If there is anything in this world I want right now it is a long, hot soak in some scented water and a chance to buff my toenails and do girly things like that. Do you mind, dear? If I retreat into my little home away from home and not see you for a little while."

He grinned and pinched her left nipple, a little tweak that Wheezy seemed to like almighty well. "Mind, darlin'? Not hardly. I need the time to recover some strength. Right

137

now I'm feelin' like Samson with his hair cut off. There just ain't much left over."

"Good. Get all your strength back, dear. If you know what I mean." If he hadn't, she managed to make it pretty clear. She laid a palm on his crotch and gave it a squeeze. Right at that moment, though, Longarm was so thoroughly used up that even that failed to get a rise from him. She kissed him again and unbolted the cabin door so he could leave.

It was just amazing to him, though, that after an afternoon of wild and acrobatic fucking, he—bigger, stronger, much more robust than frail little Eloise—he was the one who was dragging his weary ass along the deck while Wheezy was still as perky and vibrant as if she'd just risen from a nap. If he didn't know better, he would think the girl had some mystical secret by which she sapped his energy and appropriated it for her own use.

Well, he thought with a grin as he reached for a cigar, maybe she pretty much did that, at least in a manner of speaking. For sure she seemed to thrive on a steady diet of dick.

And it didn't much matter how or where that dick was applied. Wheezy seemed to like it most any way at all.

Longarm managed to make it into the gentlemen's salon without his legs giving out. The dark, paneled room was busy, filled with aromatic cigar smoke and a muted buzz of conversation. Longarm helped himself to a seat at an empty table and motioned for the waiter.

"I'll be needin' a bottle of rye whiskey, an ashtray and a deck of cards, son. Oh, and get me some small change for this, please." He laid a double eagle on the table. "Nothing bigger than a quarter."

"Yes, sir."

With those items on the table, he had no trouble tolling in enough likeminded gentlemen to make a game. Longarm was good for the evening.

Longarm was still tired when he left the gentlemen's lounge, but it was a different sort of tiredness. It was wanting sleep this time, not recovery. The truth was that despite his sleepiness he was feeling pretty damn good. Oh, he'd lost a few dollars at cards. But the gents at his table were all good company. The rye whiskey was of the finest quality. And he'd had those wonderful Hernandez y Hernandez panatelas. All in all, a very relaxing and enjoyable evening.

He headed down the stairs—ladder, dammit—to the deck below and headed, uh, aft that was it, headed toward the back of the boat, ambling along slowly and enjoying the sheen of moonlight bright on the water.

After a dozen paces or so he stopped and silently chuckled, amused with his own lapse of memory. His cabin had been way to hell and gone in the back of the boat on the *Sacagawea*. But that was last week. This time he'd been assigned to a tiny cubbyhole up toward the front. Which these crazy, damn boat folks insisted on calling the bow instead of using plain English and just saying the front.

He shook his head. Ladders, bows, sterns—it was all a mystery to him. Not that it really mattered. He could live with it if they could.

After pausing for just a moment, Longarm wheeled around to go back the way he'd just come.

Well, surprise, surprise, he thought.

There were three of them. And he didn't think they were out taking the air. Not judging by the way they reacted when he spun around like that. They all three recoiled, very much as though they expected him to attack them.

Longarm frowned. Had that shit back in St. Louis followed him onto the *Willis Adams* then? Followed him in the form of these three very large men?

They were deckhands, he guessed, or steerage passengers. Or just plain hired muscle, bullyboys earning a few easy dollars by breaking a head or a limb. Certainly no one

139

would mistake them for the genteel class of folks. They were burly, muscular sons of bitches and wore rough clothing.

By the light of a candle or low-burning lamp in a nearby cabin he could see that they wore rather calm but rigid expressions, he thought, just three good old boys out to do a job of work and earn a little fee. Although Longarm supposed that impression could be colored by this recent spate of having strangers jump him for no reason at all.

Still, he really did think they were up to no good, even though he saw no weapons in their hands, not even saps or cudgels.

Not that three guys this big would likely need weapons. He'd seen full-grown oxen with shoulders less broad and powerful than the smallest of this trio. The only advantage he had on any of them was height, as none of the three was particularly tall. On the other hand, when it came to sheer mass and muscle, these three probably outnumbered him five to one.

Sam Colt's grand equalizer could certainly eliminate their size advantage. But dammit a man doesn't like to shoot down unarmed opponents. Quite apart from what anyone else might say, something like that would suggest that he doubted himself.

And if there is one thing no peace officer can ever do it is to believe that any faint small chance exists that he might come off second best in a scrap. Once he starts doing that, he might just as well turn in his badge and buy himself a mule and plow because he will have lost his truest shield and protection.

Civilians tend to mistake that attitude for arrogance. It isn't. Instead it is a sure and certain conviction that he can whip any sonuvabitch, capture any criminal, outshoot, outfight and outrun any SOB who crosses his path. It is an ironclad belief in himself, not arrogance, that allows a good peace officer to subdue a mob single-handed . . . or to take on three big bastards like these and beat the shit out of all of them at the same time.

Besides, he calculated, as broad as these boys were they were only going to get in each other's way in this narrow passageway.

Longarm gave no more thought to the .44 at his waist. He humped his shoulders and flopped his arms a little to loosen up.

Then he waited for the three of them to come at him if that was what they damned well wanted to do.

Chapter 34

He would have whipped the bastards. All three of them. He knew damned good and well he would have.

Would have! "Would have" is as useless as "if only." But he really would have whipped them. If only.

It wasn't even that there were so many or that they were so strong, although they did outnumber him and each one of them was plenty strong.

In the close confinement of the passageway, Longarm figured he should take them. They'd have to come at him one by one, so he would put them down that same way.

Except they didn't play it that way.

Two of them squeezed in side by side, one with his left arm forward and the other with his right in position to punch. Longarm figured one of them was likely left-handed and this presented the most possible power to bring against him.

Those two standing face-to-face completely filled the passageway. They shuffled forward like they knew what they were doing. It seemed pretty clear this was a maneuver they had done before.

Even at that, he believed he could take them. After all, he had nothing against the notion of fighting dirty. There were neither rules nor referees here, and the object was survival.

The two came forward, jabbing their way in, all their blows high head shots. With two men to fight, Longarm could not calculate the usual patterns of left, right, left. They could throw left and right at the same time, and both sides with tremendous power. Longarm simply could not block everything.

He took most of the blows on his elbows and forearms. But inevitably he blocked some of those punches with his face.

Even that didn't worry him overmuch. The power of their punches, delivered with short, little grunts of effort, quickly turned his face numb and made his nose and eyes run. That was all right. He could handle that.

But—damn them to hell and back again—there weren't just those two. There were three. And in trying to ward off the pounding of the first two, he discounted the presence of the third.

That one—the son of a bitch—dropped to the deck and wormed his way past the legs of his pals.

The first thing that tipped Longarm as to what he was up against was when he lunged out and grabbed hold of Longarm's ankles.

"Shit!"

With Longarm's feet immobilized, the pair of punchers had an almost completely free hand. They pressed forward, and Longarm felt himself toppling backward.

He sprawled full-length onto the deck, lying on his back.

The three muscle boys piled onto him.

He fully expected a thrashing then. Punches, kicks—the whole gamut of pain.

Instead there was not a bit of that.

Rather than hurt him, they wrapped their arms tight around him to immobilize him and then picked him up so that he was being carried horizontally like some kicking, squirming, reluctant log.

Together, not even breathing hard, the very coordinated three men rushed him aft, toward the little observation deck at the extreme back end of the *Willis Adams*.

Longarm believed they were taking him back there where there was more room so they could finish the job of pummeling him.

He was wrong.

Damn, he was wrong.

Still carrying him like a log, they took him to the back rail and just . . . tossed him over.

Into the deadly, churning blades of the powerful stern wheel.

Longarm felt himself falling.

He was not sure. But he believed he may have screamed.

Chapter 35

Twice in the past, Longarm saw the bodies of people who had fallen into a sternwheeler's blades. They were barely recognizable as having been human by the time they were jammed through the narrow gap between the blade edges and the braces that were set so very close to those edges. The thought of winding up like that . . .

There was no time for conscious thought, only for sheer reaction. A reaction fueled by a fear that was stark but not paralyzing. If anything, the knowledge of impending disaster galvanized him.

He twisted his body so that he was falling facedown. Already lying parallel to the water—and to the wheel blades—he reached out to grab hold of a blade and pulled himself quickly to the inside of the wide slab of hard, laminated wood.

The danger lay at the outside edge of the blade where the braces were. Inside, toward the hub, was his only slim chance of survival. At the leading edge he would be so much soft material churned through a wringer. But if he could keep to the inside of the blade, if it was wide enough for him to lie on . . .

He did not know how many braces were underwater,

where a casual observer could not see them, but if he allowed any part of his body to protrude over that outside edge when the blade passed a brace, that body part would be lost and gone forever.

With that chilling thought driving him, Longarm lay on the inside of the blade and clung tight with hands, elbows, knees and feet, tighter than he'd clung to any horse he'd ever ridden. And with more serious consequences should he slip.

He gulped in a deep breath just before he felt the impact as the blade he was riding slapped hard onto the cold, unyielding water of the Mississippi.

Air bubbles obscured his vision, and swirling eddies pulled and pushed at him.

The cold shot through him like a hard, physical blow, and he had to bite back an impulse to cry out from it. But that would have robbed him of what little air that was in his lungs.

How long did it take for the huge sternwheel to pass through a revolution? He did not know. Had never cared before this moment.

Now . . . now he cared very much.

Longarm felt the power of the water trying to sweep him away from his perilously narrow ledge.

His left leg, taking the full force of the water, was ripped away from the rough wood of the blade, and Longarm's body twisted. If he lost his grip and fell free, he was a dead man. He would be crushed within seconds.

Desperately, blinded by the bubbles, pummeled by bits of trash that were floating in the river, he felt for the blade with his heel.

He thought . . . there. He hooked his heel behind the edge of the blade—why the hell hadn't he worn spurs this evening dammit—and once again lay tight against the blade.

He was disoriented. Did not know up from down or

back from front. At this moment, all he knew was that life and safety lay in making himself a part of the blade. Why hadn't they made the sonuvabitch wider anyway? Lordy!

His lungs were close to bursting. How long had he been underwater? Seconds? It seemed half a lifetime.

Heart pounding, blood pumping in his ears, terror driving him, he did not recognize it when the blade he was riding emerged into the air again on the back side of the big boat.

Then, belatedly, he realized that the water was streaming off of the blade now, off of him, and that he was surrounded by air. Sweet, blessed, wonderful air.

The blade was rising now. Lifting him high. Carrying him around for another revolution of the massive wheel.

Not damn likely.

Longarm let go of the blade and flung himself free of it, dropping quickly lest he be carried so far up that he fell into the inside of the wheel again.

His right boot hit one of the lower blades as he fell. He felt an impact as strong as any mule's kick. It spun him head over heels. He hit the water on his back, and what little air there was in his lungs was driven out again.

Jesus! There was no damn way he intended to survive that underwater ride only to drown now in open water.

Longarm jackknifed his body to right himself. And began to swim. Toward the surface. Toward the air. Toward the stars. Toward life.

Chapter 36

He came out of the water like a rat whose ship has already gone down, exhausted and soaked, crawling onto the mud and gravel of the river's bank. Once he was halfway free of the river, he collapsed, lying facedown. He stayed there and may even have drifted briefly into sleep. Or unconsciousness.

When he roused himself and sat upright again, the *Willis Adams* was long gone, disappearing upriver with no one but those three bullyboys aware that he had gone overboard.

Longarm scowled and corrected himself. Those three, and when they asked to be paid for their labors, whoever it was who hired them. Likely, he suspected, they would leave the boat at the next landing and turn back south to St. Louis to collect the balance of their assassin's pay.

Damn, but he wanted to find out who was behind these attempts on his life. And why.

As soon as he had his prisoner safely delivered to Fort Smith, dammit, Longarm intended to return to St. Louis so he could ask some questions. Maybe find one of those boys who'd jumped him this evening. All he needed was one or more of them and a little privacy. He would get the answers he wanted, or the consequences would be on their own vile heads.

For now, though, he needed to take stock. Dry out. Get up to Ferryville and finish this dreary little assignment so he could get on with the issue of the assaults. Which were, he reminded himself, attempts on the life of a federal peace officer and therefore a violation of federal law. He would be well within the scope of his job to go after the person behind all this.

Longarm was still wearing his coat. He took it off and wrung it out as best he could. At the very least it would have to be dry-cleaned and pressed. If it shrank after being immersed in the Mississippi, he would have no choice except to replace it. He scowled again. He *liked* that coat, dammit. Having to pitch it would piss him off all the more.

He seemed to be intact physically, although his right ankle hurt like a sonuvabitch and his chest felt like a bunch of small animals were nesting inside it, taking up most of the room in there. He must have swallowed a fair amount of the river.

His matches and cigars were soaked and . . . "Aw, shit!" he growled out loud. That was the second box of Hernandez y Hernandez he'd lost in as many days. His panatelas were safe and dry . . . and in his cabin aboard the *Willis Adams*. He would not be seeing those smokes again; he figured he could count on that.

The good news was that his .44 Colt was still in his holster. The leather was waterlogged and would have to be allowed to dry out before it was really usable again, and the revolver would need to be disassembled and thoroughly cleaned before oiling. Ideally, that was a job that should be done by a competent gunsmith. Longarm wanted more than a slapdash field stripping to get the Colt back in shape.

The derringer was less ticklish as to its working parts, but it could use a thorough going over also.

Clothing could be replaced easily enough, including the carpetbag and contents that remained aboard the stern-wheeler. So could his hat.

He stood up and discovered there was something else that needed replacement. His right boot was missing. It must have been knocked off by the paddle blade when he tried to jump free of the moving wheel.

He hoped the nearest town wasn't too awfully far away because he was going to have to hoof it with one foot bare unless he could attract the attention of a passing boat and beg a ride to the next place in whichever direction that outfit was traveling.

Despite the many discomforts, though, Longarm was not bellyaching. He was damned lucky to be alive after going through that meat grinder.

Sure would be nice if he could build a fire, though, to warm up beside and dry off with and attract the attention of boats on the river, too.

Yep, it would be nice. Not possible, of course. But it would be nice.

Chapter 37

Longarm felt like a scarecrow as he stepped off the decrepit little sidewheeler, the *Octavius*. A grand name for a floating pigsty. Which was no slur on the boat. The *Octavius* really was a pigsty. So to speak. The boat was used for hauling hogs. It carried mature hogs downriver to market after they were raised on the corn-rich farms in Iowa and Wisconsin.

That was a useful and no doubt profitable enterprise, Longarm realized, benefiting both the farmers, who because of it could reach markets far beyond their own rural areas, and the packing houses which provided ham and pork products to the nation's hungry citizenry. Profit, too, to the owners of the *Octavius*. All that was good, even admirable.

But, Lordy, the damn boat stank. After two days aboard, Longarm felt like the smell of it was clinging to his skin, his hair and to every piece of his stiff, brand-new clothing.

The new hat hadn't yet quite adapted itself to the shape of his head. The new boots for damn sure hadn't yet become pliable. The new holster—he still had the tried-and-true old one but it would be weeks before it would be completely dry and usable again—did not hang at quite precisely the same angle as the old. The new coat felt a mite snug across the back.

155

And he smelled, dammit, of pigs.

Despite all of that, a hint of smile tugged at his lips as he paused on the quay to light a cheap cheroot. Billy Vail's fuddy-duddy clerk Henry was going to absolutely shit when he saw Longarm's expense vouchers from this trip. Anticipating the look on Henry's face when he got a gander at those vouchers, why that made it almost worthwhile, all the crap Longarm had gone through. Almost.

He took a look around, not at all sure he'd come to the right place and never mind what he'd been told by the boss back in Denver. Ferryville, Wisconsin, looked like it would fit inside Denver's opera house and likely have room left over.

The town, what little there was of it, seemed to exist mostly because of a trio of ferries—no surprise there—to carry goods or folks across to the Iowa side of the river, which itself was considerably smaller up here than the Mississippi he was used to.

Still, this was where his prisoner was supposed to be. And the papers on the fellow had survived their dunking in a more or less legible condition. Longarm had gone to some pains to dry them out. A couple signatures had mostly disappeared from the soaking, but they should be good enough to gain custody of the guy and get him down to Fort Smith for trial. That was all that counted here.

Longarm thanked the captain of the *Octavius*, then picked up his spanking-new carpetbag and headed for the first hotel he saw. Which turned out to be the only hotel around, but that was good enough. He only needed one.

A good soak in a tub, he figured, would scrub away the hog stench. Then in the morning a haircut and a splash— make that two or three—of bay rum to finish the job.

After that he could collect his prisoner and be on his way. Easy enough.

Sure it was.

Chapter 38

The hotel clerk took a moment to scratch something deep inside his beard. Longarm wouldn't have been surprised if the man reached in there and fetched out some lice or fleas. God knew he raised a fine crop of bedbugs in his mattresses, so a few other sorts of undersized livestock would not have been cause for amazement.

Still, the place did serve a decent breakfast.

"What was that you was wanting now, mister?" the clerk asked.

"Your sheriff. Where can I find the sheriff?"

"County seat's over to Richland. That's, oh, twenty mile or so over yonder." He pointed.

"West, d'you say?" Longarm asked, taking that from the direction the man pointed.

"No, o' course not. Only thing west of here is water. And Iowa if you're of a mind to go over there. But our county seat ain't in Iowa." The clerk laughed as if he'd just made a joke.

"I thought you had someone here. A sheriff, jail, like that." Certainly this was the place Billy Vail had instructed him to go to pick up his prisoner.

The clerk dug a finger inside his beard and scratched again. "Jim Harbrough is our blacksmith. Serves as a part-time deppity, too. A little. You might wanta ask him. He's all we got for law over to this end o' the county. No call for a town marshal or jail or none of that. We're peaceable folks." The fellow grinned. "Mostly."

"Harbrough, you say? Reckon I'll ask him then. Thanks."

"You'll find Jim over to the smithy," the clerk said, although this Harbrough being the town blacksmith, Longarm just might have been able to figure that much out for himself.

The blacksmith shop was a short walk away. In Ferryville everything was a short walk away. Harbrough proved to be a short, stocky fellow with large hands and bulging muscles. He was nearly bald, although Longarm doubted he had seen the age of thirty yet.

Longarm introduced himself and stated his business.

"Oh, sure. I'm the one made the arrest. Fella came in with a horse that needed shoeing. Light saddle horse. We don't see so many of those around here. I recognized him right off from the flyers the sheriff hands around. I keep all of them, mind. Keep them in a drawer in my office, in that corner over there. This time the likeness was good, so I arrested him like I'm supposed to do and notified that U.S. marshal down in Arkansas like the flyer says to do."

"The prisoner, did he give you any trouble?" Longarm asked.

Harbrough grinned. "Not for very long, he didn't."

Longarm smiled and nodded. "If you don't have a jail, where are you keeping him? You *are* keeping him, aren't you?"

"Not me, but yes, we are keeping him. I carried him over to the county seat . . . that's at Richland . . . and turned him over to Sheriff John Dingle. Far as I know, he's still there. Unless his wife posted his bond."

"Wife? I didn't know he had a wife."

"Oh, yes. Nice little woman. She stopped here just three . . . no, it was two days ago. I think it was two. No matter. She stopped here and asked about him. I told her the same as I'm telling you. He's over in Richland in the county jail, or was the last I knew of him."

"Your sheriff surely wouldn't let him out on bail, would he?"

Harbrough's grin returned. "I don't know, Deputy. That fella's wife is awful pretty. Was she to make eyes at me, I'm not so sure I wouldn't run home and tell my wife I was gonna be gone for a few months. And I am a lay preacher in the Lutheran church here."

"I don't suppose there is any place where I can hire a horse, is there?"

"Like I already mentioned, we don't have much use for saddle horses around here. But I could rent you a buggy if you like, and a nice, fast little horse to pull it."

"The buggy will be just fine then, thank you. And directions to . . . Richland, did you say?"

"I did."

"Then I'll take the rig and directions to Richland so I can talk to Sheriff Dingle, please."

Chapter 39

It was well past noon by the time Longarm reached Richland, and at that it was a good thing there was a good horse in harness. He'd not gotten lost but more than a little confused twice on the twenty-mile trip. The roads in this staid and settled farm country were pretty disorienting to a stranger.

He did make it, though, and found the courthouse with no trouble. It was a three-story granite structure occupying a full block and fronting on the town square.

"I'm John Dingle," a graying fellow with a walrus mustache and an elk-tooth doodad on his watch chain said. "What can I do for you, friend?"

"I'm here for a prisoner in your custody. A man name of Jonas Blackburn," Longarm told him. "In custody on federal charges."

"You a lawyer or something? Not that it matters. I don't have Blackburn anymore."

"You don't . . . ?"

"Already turned him over to a United States deputy marshal."

Longarm blinked. "You what?"

161

"Did I stutter, mister? I told you. I turned Blackburn over to a U.S. deputy yesterday morning."

"A U.S. deputy," Longarm repeated.

"Mister, I don't know who the hell you are, but I wish you'd stop repeating everything I tell you. I thought I was making myself clear. A U.S. deputy marshal showed up here yesterday morning."

"Not Blackburn's wife but a deputy marshal."

"That's right. I wouldn't know about the man's wife. Although I did hear that this marshal, the lucky so-and-so, had him one awful fine-looking companion at the hotel night before last. Not that it's any of my business what a famous deputy like this one does for relaxation, you understand. None of my business."

"So there was no wife and nothing was said about bail or anything like that. Just this deputy asking to take custody of him."

"Mister, you seem just a little dense. Now, I'm sorry to say that, but it's true. I've tried to speak plain. If you want, I can go over it one more time. Yesterday morning Deputy United States Marshal Custis Long, the one who's known as Longarm to those of us in the law enforcement business, showed up in this here office. Stood right where you are standing now. Said he was here to pick up Blackburn and transport him to Fort Smith, Arkansas, to the federal court there to stand trial on charges of robbing the mail."

"Custis Long," Longarm repeated. "Known as Longarm."

"That's right. Have you heard of him?"

"I, uh . . . Yeah, Sheriff. I've heard of him. You knew this Deputy Long, did you?"

"Not before yesterday, but I have to tell you that I was mighty proud to make his acquaintance then."

"I don't suppose you asked to see his credentials," Longarm said. "Didn't ask for his badge or to see the writ of extradition for the prisoner Blackburn, did you?"

"Well, now normally I might think to do such a thing,

but this Long, you should understand that he is pretty famous inside the profession. Now, what would a hayseed sheriff from a little old farming county like ours be doing questioning someone like him, I ask you."

Longarm sighed.

He pulled out his wallet. Opened it to the badge and laid it on Sheriff John Dingle's desk.

He reached inside his coat and extracted the extradition order, unfolded it and laid that beside the wallet.

"Sheriff, you aren't gonna like this even a little bit, but I reckon you'd best look at those things. Then we'll talk some more."

Dingle gave Longarm an intensely skeptical look.

Then he bent his head to the wallet and the writ.

"Jesus Christ," he moaned a few moments later. "What have I done?"

"I think, sir, it would be fair to say that you fucked up."

Chapter 40

Someone impersonating him in order to gain custody—
custody hell, to free the son of a bitch was more like it—of
Jonas Blackburn, that pretty thoroughly explained the attacks on him in St. Louis and the one aboard the *Willis
Adams*, too.

Blackburn's gang had to get rid of Longarm in order to
keep the deception from being discovered too soon. With
any kind of luck they might figure to get away with it for
weeks, even months, before anyone was the wiser.

And undoubtedly they believed him dead now, floating
facedown in the Mississippi and likely unrecognizable,
too, after passing through the relentless grinding of that
powerful steam-driven sternwheel.

Longarm had no idea how they'd gotten on to him in
St. Louis. They might even have had someone watching
every quay on the waterfront there, looking for him, ready
to report the sighting as soon as he arrived.

It would be logical enough. After all, whether he came
overland from Denver, by boat downriver from Omaha or
up the Mississippi from the Arkansas, he was sure to pass
through St. Louis on his way to Wisconsin.

Bastards!

They thought they had a free hand now, of course.

It was a point of view Longarm intended to disprove. But . . . how? Which way would they have gone when they made their escape from Richland?

He was reasonably sure no one had gotten by him between here and Ferryville. Well, probably. He'd gotten off the road those two times when he was mildly confused as to where he was and how to get where he was going. But, dammit, he hadn't been *that* lost. Hadn't been off the proper road long enough for it to matter. Probably.

Not that he knew. Not really. From here it was all guesswork.

Longarm thanked the sheriff—not that there was any justifiable reason to do that; the man screwed up bad when he released a federal prisoner to a total stranger just on the unsupported word of a stranger—and asked where he could find a decent meal.

"I didn't take time for lunch, and I reckon this chase is going to be a long run and not a quick sprint. Seems I oughta have something to eat before I take off. One other thing, too. I need a saddle horse. Doesn't have to be especially fast but it has to have bottom. God knows how long or how hard I'll have to push it."

"There's a cafe in the next block over. The woman who runs it is called Dora. Tell her I sent you. While you're doing that," Dingle told him, "I'll get you that horse and bring it by the cafe. Do you have a saddle with you?"

"No, just this carpetbag. I'll need the saddle. And a carbine, too, if you can scare up one of those."

"Yes, I . . . that would be the least I can do. I don't suppose you could use some help tracking them down or . . . anything. Anything at all?"

Longarm was tempted to point out that the sheriff had done quite enough already. That would have been unkind, though, and pointless. The man obviously felt rotten about what he'd done.

Had every right to feel lousy about it, of course.

"No, thank you, Sheriff. I'm used to handling these things on my own. Another person to worry about would just make me leery of pulling a trigger lest it be a friendly. If I know everything in front of me is on the other side, I can shoot and not worry about it."

"It's a point of view," Dingle said reluctantly.

"You sound like you disapprove."

"It isn't that, Deputy. It's just that I don't generally have to think about things like guns. I've . . . I've never in my life had to shoot anything bigger than a snowshoe hare, knock on wood." He rapped himself on the forehead with his knuckles. "Truth is, I don't even hunt deer. I couldn't stand to shoot anything that graceful and lovely."

"Like you said," Longarm muttered, "it's a point of view." Then he smiled. "If it makes you feel any better, I hunt deer and men, too. But I've never tried to eat any of the felons I've killed, nor gut 'em either." The smile turned into a grin. "There's probably laws ag'in that."

Dingle began to look a trifle queasy. "I, uh . . . You go on over to Dora's cafe. I'll scare up that horse and bring him to you."

"You do that, Sheriff. Thank you."

167

Chapter 41

Longarm was more than a little grateful to see the cross-roads store up ahead. He was wet and hungry and thoroughly pissed off. And the horse the sheriff had given him was better suited to pulling a farm wagon than carrying a saddle.

Not long after he left Richland, the sky had turned dark and ugly, and not long after that it opened up and started pissing cold rain down the back of Longarm's neck. Among the purchases he'd made after he dragged himself out of the river, he'd missed one. He hadn't thought to get a new slicker. Now he had cause to regret the oversight.

He reined the brown horse off the road and tied it to the bole of a young mulberry tree beside the store, then stepped onto the porch and shook himself off a mite before tracking water and mud inside along with him.

"Evenin', friend. Fine weather for crops, isn't it?"

Longarm grunted and slapped his hat against his leg to knock a little more of the cold rain from it.

"What can I do for you?"

"Need to make a couple purchases, and let's start with a slicker. D'you carry any of those?"

"That I do, friend, though not the sort cut for horsemen.

The ones I sell don't have the extra oilskin at the back to cover your saddle, too. Would you want the plain slicker made for men afoot?"

"If that's what you have, then I reckon that's what I'll take. And food. I'll be needing something to eat here and now and something more to carry along with me."

"I can fix you up all right. Anything else?"

"Information would be good. I'm looking for some folks. I was supposed to meet them back in Richland, but I guess they thought I wasn't gonna show up. They left before me and I'm not sure which way they've gone."

"When was this?"

"They left Richland yesterday heading east. Driving a buggy pulled by a gray horse." He'd learned that much in Richland, from the feed and livery barn where Blackburn bought the buggy. For cash, paid in gold. He'd passed up a better rig, the feed man said, because its seat was too narrow to accommodate three. "Three people," Longarm added. "I'm not entirely sure where they're bound now that I missed catching up to them."

"Chicago," the storekeeper said.

"What's that?"

"I said your friends are going to Chicago. They asked me the best way."

"They did stop here then."

"If it's the same folks, they did, and I'd pretty much say they had to've been your friends. I can go months at a time without seeing a face that's new to me. Now I've had strangers two days in a row. Imagine that."

"Yes. Imagine that. What was it they bought from you?" Longarm asked.

The storekeeper pursed his lips. "Now, I don't know as I ought to be telling you things like that. I mean, a fellow's purchases can be private. You know?"

Longarm opened his wallet to display the badge. "Not all that private, I think."

"Oh, my. This here is official, is it?"

"Yes, sir, it surely is. Federal. It's important."

"Oh, my." The man shook his head. "Oh, dear."

"You aren't in any trouble, mister. But I need your help. Now tell me what you can, please."

"Well there was the three of them, of course. The two men and that little girl. She surely isn't involved in anything untoward, is she? I mean, she seemed so . . . angelic, I suppose I would say. And her so young and pretty and a cripple."

"A cripple?" Longarm asked.

"Well, I suppose she would be called that. With her bad leg, I mean. There's something wrong with her leg so that she doesn't walk exactly right. Makes her dip and sway when she walks. I felt sorry for her." He sighed. "So pretty."

Longarm felt a chill that had nothing to do with the rain that soaked him. Eloise Stephens. Wheezy!

That explained . . . pretty much everything, didn't it?

No damn wonder the would-be assassins got on to him so quickly back in St. Louis. He was fucking the person who hired his murder. Shee-damned-it!

Out of funds, was she? Like hell. She wanted an excuse to stay close to him so she could tip the hired hands how to reach him.

And no damned wonder she'd put a bullet in that fellow who broke into their room at the hotel. She hadn't wanted him captured alive and turning on her under questioning.

Longarm felt like an idiot. Wheezy.

She would also have been the dutiful little wife Jim Harbrough mentioned back in Ferryville. Longarm hadn't made the connection then. Now it was inescapable. Eloise Stephens was in league with Blackburn. Girlfriend, wife—it didn't matter. She had him out of jail. Her plan had worked, dammit. Worked all too well.

"Yesterday, you said they were here."

"That's right. A little earlier than this time of day. Early afternoon, call it. They bought a few things off of me. Asked directions, like I said. And they asked for a place where they could lay over even though it was still early. One of the things they bought, though, was a bottle of whiskey. I got the impression they were celebrating something."

"They were," Longarm said without explaining further. "But I don't think they'll be celebrating for long."

"You trying to catch them, are you?"

"I surely am."

The fellow nodded toward the front door to his store. "Looks like you're in luck then."

"How's that?"

"The rain. If this keeps up, the roads are all going to be nothing but mud. Them being in that driving rig and you being on horseback, you'll catch them easy. If the rain keeps up."

Longarm managed a smile for the first time in quite a while. "Drag out that slicker, will you. And a little something to put in my belly."

"You going back out in this right away, are you?"

"Yes, sir, I expect that I am. Oh, and one more thing if you would. I'd like to know which route you told them to take."

"Glad to help, Officer. Yes indeed, glad to help," the storekeeper said as he began gathering things and piling them onto the counter, starting with a bright yellow oilskin slicker.

Chapter 42

Longarm pushed the brown throughout much of the night, only stopping in the small hours to allow the horse some rest from the clinging mud. The beast was not fast, but it was sturdy enough and there was no quit in it. He had to give it credit for that much.

He found a tree-lined stream at the foot of one of the countless rolling hills in this part of the country, and stopped there for what remained of the night. He made a cold camp—there seemed little choice about that since the rain had thoroughly drenched everything he could find— and let the horse pick at the lush grasses along the creek bank while Longarm pulled the slicker close around him and tried to make himself comfortable. That was a losing proposition, for the rain continued to fall and he was already wet to the skin after leaving Richland without a slicker. He was more than a little pleased to see a thin, gray pallor in the eastern sky.

"Must be morning," he muttered aloud.

With a little light to see by, he dug into his new saddle-bags for a can of tomatoes and used his belt knife to pierce the top so he could drink off a little of the tartly acidic juice, then cut the can the rest of the way open and broke some squares of hardtack in with the tomatoes.

He kept waiting for the tomato juice to soften the hardtack. It didn't. Amazing stuff these biscuits. They were pretty much indestructible. Longarm figured these particular ones were probably left over from the war. The War of 1812 would've been his guess.

The dreadful stuff filled his belly, though, and gave him the impression of warmth, never mind that the impression was a bald-faced lie.

Done with his breakfast, he took a quick shit, washed in the creek and saddled the brown, ready for another assault on the mud and slop that passed for a road around here.

It was late in the morning when Longarm spotted what he believed to be his quarry stuck axle-deep in the road ahead. Bad as the going was mounted on this horse, it must have been far, far worse in the light buggy.

Longarm was not about to ride up to the rig without looking the situation over beforehand. He reined off to one side and up the slope of yet another hill that lay parallel to the road. Once he was away from the road, he was no longer looking at the back of the buggy and could get a better look at the rig.

There was no horse hitched to it. The poles lay empty in the mud. And there was no sign of any of the three people who had been riding in it.

He paused to take a look to either side but saw no danger. And after all, Blackburn and friends would not think there was any immediate threat behind them. As far as they knew, Longarm was dead, crushed or drowned back in the Mississippi, and not enough time had yet passed to make Billy Vail or the officers attached to the Arkansas court suspicious. At this point the three should think they were loose and running free.

Except for being mired knee deep in Wisconsin mud.

Longarm held the brown to the side of the road where

the footing was better and approached the empty buggy. When he reached it, he saw why the fugitives abandoned it. Not only were the wheels trapped in the mud, the front axle was busted as well.

Lousy driving, probably. Longarm figured they may have tried to drive on after dark and paid for the mistake with that broken axle.

There were three pieces of luggage lashed on the cargo board at the back of the buggy. He recognized them easily enough. They were Wheezy's bags, the one she had taken with them to the hotel back in St. Louis and some of the bags—the important ones, he supposed—she had left with the ticket broker while they were waiting for the *Willis Adams* to arrive.

She was a hell of a girl, that Wheezy. Good enough to fool his hairy ass, although until she came along he would have sworn that was impossible.

He tipped his head back and squinted up at the gray and dripping sky. There was no sign of any letup in the rain. But hell, he was getting used to it by now.

He reached inside the slicker and produced one of the cheap and perfectly vile little crooks he was reduced to smoking until he could find something decent, bit the twist off, then reached inside the slicker for a match.

The trick now would be to get the match aflame and the cigar lighted.

When he bent his head, he saw a flicker of bright yellow flame off on the hillside to his right.

A moment later he heard the bee-drone zip of a bullet going past and a moment after that the dull booming report of a gunshot.

Longarm threw himself off the brown horse and sprawled belly-down in the mud.

Chapter 43

Sonuvabitch gun wouldn't come out of the sonuvabitch holster and then the sonuvabitch hammer hung up on one of the slicker's buttons and he was mud from head to sonuvabitch toes and this was not no damn *fun*!

The guy on the hillside fired again, and this time Longarm got a good look at the clump of brush he was hiding in.

He finally managed to drag his Colt out and cock it—not strictly necessary since the .44 was a double-action revolver, but better for a slow squeeze and steady aim—and sighted carefully at the base of the brush. Sumac, he thought, not that it mattered.

Longarm used the back of his thumb to wipe the mud away from his eyes, tugged his hat low to better protect him from the rain and very gently squeezed the trigger.

His Colt bellowed and bucked in his hand, and over on the hillside fifty or so yards away he heard a dull thump and a soft cry.

Either he'd hit the bastard . . . or the guy wanted Longarm to think that he had. Fifty yards is a long shot for a short gun, but accuracy at that range is more a matter of steadiness of hand and shortness of sight radius than anything else. Revolver or rifle, either one, a bullet will not drop enough at that distance to really worry about.

The thing was, Longarm really was not sure.

He cocked the Colt and very carefully squeezed off another one. This time he neither heard nor saw anything in response. Which told him precisely nothing.

"Shit," he mumbled quietly to himself, while he shucked his empties and reloaded the two chambers.

He lay there, wet and cold and thoroughly pissed off, for a good ten minutes. Or maybe it was five. After all, nobody put a clock on it. The point was, he lay there until he wasn't in any mood to do it a second longer, then held the Colt at the ready and rolled suddenly to the side. Away from the brown horse, which despite the gunfire was standing steady as a rock. The horse hadn't moved since Longarm leaped off.

Not that he was paying attention to the horse. He was watching that hillside. And not just the sumac where the shooter had been a few minutes earlier. By now the guy could well have moved.

No one shot at him. Nothing moved except the raindrops that continued to spatter onto the mud.

Longarm felt cold and clammy, and like he'd been bathing in mud. People paid good money to immerse themselves in mud, he was told. Now that he'd had the experience, he could not for the life of him understand why.

He crouched and scuttled sideways, darted forward, crabbed over to the side again. Zigzagging back and forth, he advanced up the hillside like a good cow pony sneaking up on an old mossback cow, making a big show of going sideways and hoping the uphill motion wouldn't be noticed.

Fifteen, twenty minutes later, he was level with the sumac clump and could get a look behind it.

Someone was there, but the guy was not interested in

doing any more shooting. He'd had a revolver that now lay on the ground at his side. His hands were locked together high on his belly.

"You over there. You still alive?"

Longarm saw the man's head nod.

"Don't reach for your iron or I'll put one in the side of your head."

The fellow shook his head. Very carefully, as if he were afraid it might topple off his shoulders if he got too energetic about it.

Longarm came fully upright and stepped behind the bole of a tree so he could give the rest of the hillside a looking over before he made a silly mistake by assuming the guy was alone before he was sure of it. He also removed the bright yellow slicker. The thing made him feel conspicuous as hell standing there.

After looking, he hiked. Uphill, around in a circle and back down again, so that he approached the ambusher from the other direction.

As far as he could tell the shooter'd been alone.

"I'll be damned," Longarm said. "You're still breathing."

The guy looked at him without expression. Longarm recognized him. He had been one of the three bullyboys aboard the *Willis Adams.*

"I thought we'd kilt you," the tough guy whispered.

"You was wrong."

The man's face twisted, although whether that was in pain or from the disappointment of not having killed Longarm when they threw him into the sternwheel, Longarm could not be sure.

"If you thought I was dead," Longarm asked, "why the ambush?"

"Wasn't no . . . ambush. I was . . . left here. By the bastard . . . Blackie an' his bitch."

"Left here?"

"Sumbish shot me. Inna gut. You think you coulda took me if I hadn't already been half gone? Not on . . . your best fucking . . . day."

"Yeah, sure. I believe you, pal."

"Doesn't matter now."

"No, it doesn't. You're a dead man for sure," Longarm said pleasantly.

"Cheerful fucker . . . ain't you."

"As long as it's you has the bullet in his belly and not me, sure. So where are Blackburn and Wheezy?"

The man turned his head and indicated with his chin in a direction Longarm thought was southeast. "Gone to . . . Chicago."

"What's in Chicago?"

"The high life. Till the money . . . runs out. Blackie is . . . like that. So's the bitch."

"They've done this before then?"

"Except for gettin' caught an' 'cept for . . . shooting me . . . yeah."

"Tough deal, eh?"

"Yeah. Listen. Do me . . . favor . . . will you?"

"It depends," Longarm told the dying man.

"Send a letter . . . to my mama. Tell her some . . . some shit about it. You know. I was a good boy. Died tryin' to . . . save some sonuvabitch's sorry ass. Saved somebody from drowning. Some . . . shit like that. Make something up. Will you do that?"

"It depends. Will you do a favor for me in return?"

"Hell . . . yes. Why not, huh?"

"Then give me your right name and your mama's name and address. Then I want you to answer some questions. If you do that and I find you've told me the truth, I'll send that letter and make your mother proud of you."

The muscular fellow nodded and managed a smile. "All ri-right. You got you a . . . deal, mister."

180

Chapter 44

Longarm wasn't easily impressed, but this place damn sure managed to do it.

He stood in the hotel lobby, again wearing new clothing, after that last batch was ruined by mud and water, and positively gawked.

The lobby was four stories high, with a domed ceiling made of stained glass, gilded columns supporting balconies above the ground floor and in the center of the marble floor a fountain. An actual, fucking fountain. Indoors. With cherubs and half-naked women and two of those funny-looking creatures—he couldn't remember what they were called—that were half-man and the bottom half goat.

He could not imagine what it would cost to stay in a place like this. Ten dollars a night? Twenty? Shee-it!

"May I help you, sir?" The fellow asking wore a cutaway coat and a collar so tall and tight that looked like it would cut his throat if he turned his head too fast. He had a prissy look about him. It seemed pretty clear that he disapproved of this six-gun-wearing ruffian in his lobby. It was perfectly all right if he didn't approve of Longarm, though. Longarm didn't much like him or his attitude either.

"Looking for a friend," Longarm said without deigning to turn his head enough to look at the man.

"May I have his name, sir?"

"No."

"I must insist, sir."

"Get fucked."

The fellow looked like he was going to faint dead away. "Sir! Please. I am afraid I must ask you to leave now."

Longarm turned to face him and took half a step forward so that the point of his chin was almost touching the bridge of the hotel man's nose. "You are interfering with a peace officer in the performance of his duties. I can arrest you for that. In fact I *will* arrest you for that if you don't leave me the fuck alone. Are we clear?"

The man stumbled backward. "I . . . I . . ."

"Go away," Longarm said. "Go bother somebody else."

The hotel man turned and scurried away. Longarm ambled across the broad, polished floor and picked up a copy of the day's *Chicago Times* and carried it to one of the settees provided for the comfort of guests. He chose a spot that gave him a view of the entire lobby, the gracefully curving staircase and the cage of the mechanical lift thing, elevator they called it. Unnatural, Longarm thought. He had no desire to ride one of the things. They didn't look safe.

He opened the newspaper to one of the inside pages and laid it in his lap, removed his Stetson and set it aside so he would not be quite so conspicuous in these fancy-dan surroundings, then settled down to wait. And to watch.

"Table for one, sir?" the dining room headman asked. Maître d', he'd be called? Something like that, Longarm thought.

"No, thank you. I see some friends over there. I'll be joining them."

"Then if I may have your name, sir, I shall announce you to them."

"That won't be necessary."

"I must insist, sir. It would not be correct for you to join their party without an invitation."

"Oh, I'm a party crasher from way back, so don't you worry about it." Longarm looked over the top of the fellow's head to a table in the far corner where Jonas Blackburn and Eloise Stephens were just being served their shirred eggs and croissants along with strawberries and cream. It was all quite elegant and refined. "Excuse me now, friend. I'm just gonna have a word with those folks over there."

"Sir, you cannot . . ."

But Longarm paid no mind to him and was already striding purposefully across the dining room, which was nearly empty at this late hour.

Blackburn looked up with a questioning look. He had never in his life laid eyes on Custis Long, though, and exhibited no alarm. "Yes?"

Longarm stopped behind Wheezy, who had not bothered to look around. "Vacation's over, Jonas. It's time you put the handcuffs on again so's we can head down to Fort Smith."

Blackburn became pale. "You are . . ."

"Long," Longarm said. "Deputy United States marshal."

That damn sure got Wheezy's attention. She spun sideways in her chair and gave him a stricken look.

"Hello, darlin'," Longarm said. "It seems I'm not quite as dead as you thought I was."

"But . . . they said . . . You weren't on the boat. You . . ."

"Yeah, I missed you, too, little dear, but I've found you again and isn't that just fine. We'll have plenty of time to talk over old times. But don't you worry, darlin'. I don't expect they'll hang you. Why, being such a pretty little bit of a thing, you might get out in twenty years or so." The words and the smile were for Wheezy, but his attention was on Blackburn, who Longarm expected was very apt to resist arrest.

That, dammit, was a mistake. Longarm realized it almost too late. Wheezy reached for the little beaded handbag lying beside her plate. She opened it quite casually, with no apparent urgency. He thought she was reaching for a handkerchief or something of that nature.

Instead he saw a glint of metal when she brought her hand out of the bag.

He saw the bright gleam of the dining room lights reflecting on a nickel-plated pistol.

Longarm did not take time to think about it. He simply reacted.

As Wheezy swung the muzzle of the pistol toward him, her thumb already tugging the hammer back, Longarm swept his Colt out, finger squeezing even before the barrel came on line with its target.

It was the Colt .44 that fired first, the roar of its muzzle blast filling the spacious dining room and sending the few others there into a state of immobilizing shock.

Wheezy's little gun spat, too, when her finger reflexively jerked, but its bullet came nowhere near him, winding up harmlessly in one of the dining room walls.

Longarm's slug struck the beautiful blond girl high in the chest, just below the tender hollow at the base of her throat, a spot Longarm had kissed so many times while they were together, while Wheezy was spying on him and plotting to have him murdered, a spot that was marred now by a gout of blood pouring out of her body and soiling her lovely gown.

She was flung backward, falling off the chair with a crash of breaking china and the clatter of cutlery as she took the tablecloth and their brunch with her.

The pistol—an Ivor Johnson, Longarm noticed—had

fallen as well. He kicked it aside, his attention returned now to Blackburn.

"Are you in, Jonas?"

"I . . . no. Not me. I am not armed. Not here."

"Stand up then. Take your coat off. I'll be wanting to make sure you don't have no fangs. Then we'll take us a little trip down to Arkansas."

"What about Eloise?"

Longarm glanced down. The girl was still alive, her mouth—God, he remembered that mouth all too well and the marvelous things she could do with it—her mouth open, gulping like a trout on a creek bank, seeking air that had no passageway now. Maybe she was asphyxiating; maybe she was drowning. It really did not matter which. "She won't be coming with us, Jonas."

"May I hold her? Comfort her one last time? Please?"

Longarm glanced at the silver pistol. It was well out of reach. He nodded, and Blackburn hurried around the table and dropped to his knees, taking Wheezy's head into his lap and cradling her there quite tenderly.

Theirs must have been a mighty strange relationship, Longarm thought, but who was he to say that it hadn't been love? Certainly Jonas Blackburn's tears were real enough.

But then Longarm almost felt like shedding some himself.

The girl had been very special. Beautiful and accomplished. He supposed he would never know what all she really had been.

He was not sure exactly when it was that she died. He was not in any hurry now anyway. He pulled a chair up—there were plenty of them available now as the dining room had completely emptied in the past couple minutes—and let Blackburn grieve. There was ample time now to get down to Arkansas.

All the damn time in the world.

Watch for

LONGARM AND THE MISSING MISTRESS

the 322nd novel in the exciting LONGARM series
from Jove

Coming in September!

LONGARM

Explore the exciting Old West with one of the men who made it wild!

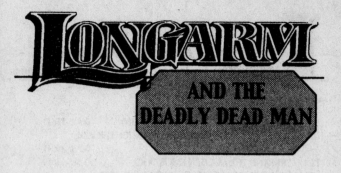

LONGARM

AND THE DEADLY DEAD MAN

IN THIS GIANT-SIZED ADVENTURE,
AN OUTLAW LEARNS THAT HE'S
SAFER IN HIS GRAVE THAN
FACING AN AVENGING ANGEL
NAMED LONGARM.

0-515-13547-X